STRANGE AND DISTURBING

STRANGE AND DISTURBING

13 Late Night Campfire Tales

TERRY DALY KARL

Strange and Disturbing is a work of fiction. Names, characters, and incidents are a product of the author's imagination or used fictionally. Any resemblance to actual persons or events is entirely coincidental.

Copyright © Terry Daly Karl
All rights reserved

ISBN: 1534756639
ISBN 13: 9781534756632

DEDICATION

*To my dear husband, Jeff,
for listening to my stories
with patience and
helpful advice.*

Special Thanks to:
The Grainy Girls:
Amy
Krysta
Kori
Toni

CONTENTS

Incident at the Hanson Farm · 1
Watch Out for the Wild · 12
He Comes in the Night · 25
Dealing with the Devil · 34
Bon Appetit · 44
A Hunting We Will Go · 48
I Think, Therefore, I Am · 56
A Gift from the Faerie Prince · 64
The Man Who Could Walk Through Walls · · · · · · · · · · · 80
The Chicken Foot Talisman · 91
The Madhouse · 100
DNA Secrets · 108
Madam Blotsky · 114

About the Author · 127

INCIDENT AT THE HANSON FARM

The Hanson farm was small and in decline. It stood unassuming in its ordinariness at the end of a long dirt driveway tucked in between two very large hills, somewhere in a remote area of the Allegany Foot Hills. The house was L-shaped and had a rickety front porch across the front. Hunks of white paint were missing off the clapboard siding. Three small decrepit outbuildings and a large, mostly red, barn were also located on the property. In other words, it looked pretty much like every other poor farm in the area, with nothing to distinguish it from its neighbors except for the strange lights and low humming noise that emanated from the barn in the middle of every August.

Linus Hanson was the owner of this, less-than-notable, farm. He was a rough man in his late fifties, strong for his age, as farmers usually are, and he was ugly. His face was craggy and worn from a life of hard labor; worry and the lack of good dental work was evident; there was the stamp of the kind of wrinkles you always found on the face of a person who was inordinately mean. Yes, Linus was ugly. He was ugly all the way clean to the bone.

He was well known in the town for his mean nature and bad attitude, and everyone thought he was crazy. Not just a little strange, but down right crazy, as his father had been before him. "Those Hansons," the townsfolk would say. "They're not right."

He had a wife, Gert. Nobody hardly knew she existed. She was about as noticeable as his farm, graying brown hair, brown eyes, meek and mild.

His son, Jasper, was a chip off the old block. He was mean to his mother, mean to all the girls at school, and mean to his sister. He did whatever his father told him, with no sass back, mostly because, he didn't want to be on the wrong end of his father's ire; But he hated his father too. The truth was, he was just scared of him.

His daughter, Laura Jean, was a pretty thing. Fair of face and fair of hair, she didn't look like either of her parents. Perhaps, she resembled a grandparent or some other, long dead, ancestor. And her temperament was strong, not meek like her mother. But still, she had her own issues that tarnished, what could have been, a fine personality.

On a particularly hot evening in mid-August, at the time of year when the Hanson farm usually turned strange, Linus was feeling out-of-sorts. He had just eaten a fine meal that Gert had prepared, and he should have been content. But, to his mind, the mashed potatoes were cold, and the beef was too chewy for his discriminating palate, and he had just finished off his last beer, because he had managed to drink the entire twelve pack. His stomach was rumbling in an unpleasant manner, and his beer-high was crashing to an uncomfortable condition, and everyone was starting to irritate him.

"I don't know how you expect me to eat shit like that," he barked over at Gert. "I work hard all day, and I get crap for dinner."

Gert said nothing. She had learned through the years that trying to defend herself would only get her a crack across the mouth. She worried that this was going to be 'one of those nights'. Her own dinner started to turn into a lump in her belly. She tried to make herself small and invisible in the corner of the kitchen.

"Why don't you leave Ma alone," Laura Jean spoke up, knowing already that it was a mistake, but she had a bit of defiance in her, something inherited from a grandparent, perhaps,—but in a good way—and she was tired of watching her mother never sticking-up for herself. She felt it was her role in the family to always be the peacemaker.

"What was that, missy?" Her father's eyes lost focus on Gert and narrowed in her direction.

Laura Jean's bravery started to wane, or maybe, she was just coming to her senses, but she decided to soften her voice. "You heard me."

Linus reached out and grabbed her by the arm. He pulled his ugly face to within an inch of hers. "Don't test me, girl. Not tonight, of all nights. Do you know what horrors are coming? Do you? Do you? ... Well I do."

His spit sprayed onto her face, and she could smell his dinner and years of bad teeth. God, he was revolting. She set her lips in a tight line and stared back at him with a stubborn look.

"Yeah, you always tell us how you faced *it* down. What a brave man you are. ... Brave, my ass. You're sittin' here drinkin' yourself stupid, like you always do at this time of year. Over what? We ain't never seen nothin' out there in the barn. Your stories are all full of shit! And *you're* all full of shit!"

A purple kind of flush bloomed over his face; his eyes shrunk down to slits; he gritted his teeth. She'd done it now. She was going to be in for something really bad. Everyone in the room held their breath.

"I'm full of shit, huh? Well you're going to find out, missy. Tonight, you're going to ... find ... out."

Linus twisted his daughter's arm until she cried out. He dragged her over to the door and pushed her through. "Get over there to the barn, girl. You get over there, and you spend the night there. Don't you dare come back here 'till morning or, by God, I'll whup the tar out of you. Give me sass, will you? We'll see how brave you are in the morning."

Laura Jean stood in the middle of the back yard glowering at her father. God, she hated him. She wished she was a strong man right now. She'd go over there and beat his ass. She'd punch him, and kick him, and punch him some more. It would feel so good to put him down. ... But she wasn't big, and she wasn't strong.

She could see in his eyes that he wanted her to come crawling back, beg his forgiveness, rather than go into the barn. He thought he had her where he wanted her. His eyes were wet with the pleasure it was giving him.

From behind her enraged father, she could see her mother and brother peeking out of the windows at the back of the porch. Their faces looked scared. Laura Jean stared at them and pleaded silently with her eyes, but she was on her own. One by one, they looked down and turned away. She was the only one with any backbone, she thought, sadly. There would be no help from them. Defiantly, she raised her chin and turned toward the barn.

"I'll walk into Hell before I give you the satisfaction!" she yelled over her shoulder. Then she marched angrily toward the barn ... and *Hell* itself, for all she knew.

The barn was already beginning to glow. She could hear a low hum thrumming from that direction. Through the soles of her feet, she could feel a faint vibration in the earth. And there was a smell of brimstone in the air. She had never been inside the barn on the night of mid-August. She had always stayed away. The whole family had always stayed away. Her father claimed to have seen *it* when he was young—the cause of the glow and the low hum—but it was too horrible for him to talk about. Now, perhaps, she was going to find out for herself. She could face what was in the barn, or she could turn and walk back to the house, in shame, to face her father.

Screw that! She decided she'd take her chances with the barn. But, although she was determined, her steps slowed as she got closer to the barn, her knees got weaker and weaker with each step.

Laura Jean opened the door to the barn. It took all the courage she could find in her heart. She knew that her father was terrified to go anywhere near the barn in mid-August, but he never did say why. She tried to swallow, but her mouth had gone dry.

How bad could it be? Nothing ever seemed to happen to the barn during this event. The barn would look strange for a few hours, and then everything would return to normal.

Laura Jean looked around. Everything inside was glowing. Everything was humming. As she stared, it grew brighter. Her chest tightened with panic, and she ran over to the corner and hid behind a stall wall, hoping that whatever was in here wouldn't see her there.

Time past. It seemed to Laura Jean that it was forever. She noticed that her arms and legs were shaking, and she tried to slow her breathing down so she wouldn't make any noise. ... Then she heard something moving in the opposite corner.

Oh, my God! What is it? I'm going to die!

She didn't want to, but she looked around the corner anyway. She couldn't stop herself. Her curiosity had gotten the better of her. Besides, if you were going to die, she thought, you might as well know what killed you.

In the far corner, where she had thought she'd heard the sound, the light was even brighter. And there was a spot, kind of shaped like a rectangle, where the light was so bright it hurt her eyes. It was almost too bright to look at. She put one of her shaking hands over her eyes to tone down the glare, squinting to try and see what might be lurking at the other end of the barn.

A shadow took shape in the incredible brightness. Actually, it was something that was a little less bright than the background ... and it was moving.

Her reactions frozen, almost unable to breathe, she stared in growing horror as she realized the shadow was moving closer toward her. It was coming straight at her. She knew she wouldn't be able to make it to the door, even if she could find the courage to finally move. And Laura Jean also realized that, at some point ... she had begun to pray.

Eventually, the shape moved directly in front of her, and it blocked out most of the blinding light behind it. Whatever it was, it didn't look quite human. It stood on two legs, and it had a head, but she wasn't sure if what she saw on that head was a face. Her mind didn't know how to recognize what she was seeing. Its skin appeared to be gray in color, and the skin was definitely moving and shimmering like the surface of water. It was like nothing she had ever encountered before. At first, she was too stunned to react, but when she opened her mouth to scream ... nothing came out.

The figure hunkered down in front of her. She thought she heard, *don't be afraid*. But then she realized there was no voice. The sound—if you could call it that—was in her head. She felt weak, and vulnerable, and violated.

"What the hell are you?" she whispered.

It held out a long thin arm, on the end of which was a hand—of a sort—with four long digits that extended toward her. And then it waited.

Laura Jean felt revulsion and fear, and curiosity and wonder. Was she supposed to take its hand? Ugh. Then she would have to touch it. She, obviously, couldn't get away from it. ... Maybe she could try. Maybe she could knock it over and make a beeline for the door. It didn't seem to be very big. She tried to move and realized her legs were still paralyzed with fear, and suddenly she was filled with uncontrollable panic.

As terrible visions of the nasty things this creature might have in store for her flashed before her eyes, she looked down at her arm, and she saw, with extreme horror, that without her even realizing it, she was raising up her hand toward the outstretched tip of the inhuman finger.

We find you acceptable.

Unbidden, her mind was filled with these words. She didn't know where these thoughts were coming from, but she was powerless to look away from the terrifying creature, powerless to close her mind to the visions invading her thoughts. In her mind's eye, she could see the encounter this being had had with her father so many years ago. She could remember that meeting as if she had been there herself. She could sense the revulsion the being had felt as it had entered the angry and petulant mind of her father. And she could sense the reaction of loathing that her father had experienced.

"He was not worthy," she whispered. "Oh, my God, he was not worthy. No wonder he's been bitter all these years."

She looked at the alien in front of her with new understanding. She was beginning to believe that it meant her no harm. It had been coming here every year for as long as she could remember, and there had never been any harm done to anyone. Her fear of the barn was the result of her father's fear. Laura Jean resolved to think for herself.

We mean you no harm, the voice in her head said. *We wish only to learn.*

The alien patiently waited, its arm extended, as if it had all the time in the world. With a growing curiosity she could not quell, Laura Jean moved her hand one more inch closer toward the outstretched hand of the luminous creature before her. She took a breath, her heart pounding, and then she made contact.

"I, also, wish to learn."

At the instant of physical contact, Laura Jean understood *everything*. Gone was the frightened girl huddled in the corner of the barn. Gone was the timid daughter of the overbearing farmer. At that moment, she realized that her father meant nothing in the grand scheme of the universe. He was small and insignificant. The farm was insignificant. She, herself, was insignificant in the vast expanse of space and time. And yet, to her wonder, she realized that she was a part of it. She was part of the great universe, part of everything that was, and everything that will be. And she was an *important* part of everything, as all life and matter was. At that moment, she was filled with a profound sense of peace and happiness, a contentment like she had never known.

The thought came into her head, *do you want to come with us?*

With the new knowledge the being had shared with her, Laura Jean no longer felt any fear of the alien. And she, also, felt no need to remain in this land of ignorance and pain. She felt more valued and more special than she ever had before. And so, without hesitation or reservation, she answered, "Yes." Then she rose up from behind the wall and followed the being's retreating form toward the brilliant light radiating from the opposite corner of the barn.

"Yes," she said. "And, thank you."

As she entered the light, in her new state of euphoria, Laura Jean looked around her with mild interest at the unusual array of metal probes.

That hot summer night in mid-August Laura Jean Hanson, daughter of Linus and Gert Hanson, went missing. She was missed at school. She was missed at the restaurant where she worked part time. She was missed by her—on again, off again—boyfriend. And she was missed by at least one member of her family.

When asked about her whereabouts, her father said that she had run off. But he knew where she had gone. *It* had taken her. He was sure as hell, that creepy little bastard had nabbed his daughter. The thing had tried to take him too once, he remembered, but then it had changed its mind. He might have intuited the phrase, *inferior specimen,* but he knew that he was just damn lucky. And if he started to feel guilty about sending Laura Jean to the barn, he would remind himself that she'd deserved it. The little bitch.

Her mother and her brother went along with whatever Linus said. They were both weak-willed and timid. And, truthfully, they really weren't sure what had happened to Laura Jean. They really didn't want to know.

The townsfolk were suspicious. They didn't think the girl had run off, and they knew Linus had a reputation for having a vicious temper. Besides, they all knew he was crazy. The local police started keeping a closer eye on everyone at the farm, but they never learned what happened to Laura Jean, and they never found a body.

As time passed, Linus got even uglier and even meaner. Eventually, Linus was arrested for wife beating and put in prison. He died there, himself, ironically, taking a beating from another prisoner.

Gert Hanson remained on the farm her whole life. What else could she do? That was her life; though her life was a lot happier after they put Linus in jail.

Jasper Hanson inherited the farm when his mother died, and though he always claimed to have hated his 'old man', he grew up to be just like him.

The family lives there still to this day. But no one, except the family, ever comes around. The townsfolk are sure the place is haunted.

"Those Hansons," they'll say. "Why, they're crazy. You don't want to go anywhere near that Hanson place. Especially, not in mid-August, on the anniversary of the night Laura Jean disappeared. That's when her ghost walks the place. That's when her wraith wanders. That's when her shimmering form, still in the bloom of youth, comes to visit the farm. It's then you can see the strange lights. And it's then you can hear the low hum vibrating the earth, like the otherworldly moaning of a long dead teenager.

"You don't want to go near that Hanson place," They'll say. "And whatever you do ... stay away from the barn."

WATCH OUT FOR THE WILD

Frank Barrett was relieved when he turned onto 416 going north. It had been a beautiful morning, but the sun was in his eyes all the way down 401. Ever since he crossed into Canada at the Thousand Islands Bridge and started driving east, the glare had been burning into his eyes. He was beginning to get a headache. But now with the sun to the side, he could stop squinting, and he glanced over at the clock. It was still early, so he was making good time. He'd probably be in the city by 11:00 o'clock. That would give him an hour to find the restaurant, so it should be no problem. He had the directions, and he had his GPS.

Gretchy would be waiting for him at the Senator's Inn Restaurant in Ottawa at 12:00. And there, he was to meet Marielle Charbonneau. She was the woman who owned the cottage on Lac-Belle where Gretchy had seen the 'unusual tracks'. He could hardly wait to hear her story.

STRANGE AND DISTURBING

Frank's interest had been peaked about these tracks since the day before yesterday, when he had called his good friend Gretchy, a close buddy of his from his days—not more than two years ago now—at Syracuse University. She had been working for the Conservation Department at Gatineau Provincial Park in Quebec, a wonderful position that she had gotten right after graduation, while he, unfortunately, was still looking for a permanent job.

Sadly, there were not as many ready openings in journalism. Either that, or he wasn't looking in the right places. The only way he was using his degree was by writing short freelance articles, every now and then, for the Watertown Gazette. He told himself, that he was writing a book about New York politics, but since he'd only gotten about twenty-five pages complete before he had hit a brick wall, he found that he had completely lost interest in the subject.

He needed to be working on something, he decided, until he got his big break. So, yesterday, while reading the latest issue of the Gazette, he had found an article, on page three, about the disappearance of three campers from the Gatineau Park. There was an aside in the article about two other people who had gone missing in the nearby area of Sainte-Cecile-de-Masham in the last six months, though the inspectors didn't believe that the previous cases were, in any way, connected to this new situation.

That, by itself, could be the basis for an interesting story, he thought, but Frank's cluttered brain had coughed up the remark he had heard his friend Gretchy make the other night. If he put the two stories together, he might be able to come up with something really eye-catching. It might even get picked-up by the Associated Press. He remembered, that even before he had learned about the disappearances, he had been intrigued by Gretchy's tale. The two of them were having a phone conversation about the good old days, while he was pounding down a few beers at the Watering Hole, a little dive on State Street in downtown Watertown, and she had commented about some strange prints she had seen in the dirt around her friend's cottage. She had said that this cottage, which was converted from an old hunting lodge, was located on the northeast shore of Lac-Belle. Frank knew that Lac-Belle was just north of the sites of all the disappearances.

She had thought the tracks looked like dog prints or wolf prints, only they were incredibly large. The animal would have had to weigh upwards of sixty-five kg; that would be almost one hundred and forty five pounds, she'd said, too large for the average dog. And in some places she could see only back paw prints in the ground, as though the animal had been walking on two legs. He had felt a shiver run down his spine as she told him about it. She said, she believed it was a ... what did she call it? ... A loup-garou. Yes, that's what she said it was, a loup-garou: some kind of mythical beast.

Not that Frank believed in that kind of thing, but now his imagination was starting to churn around in his head. Why not go up to Canada, talk to his friend Gretchy, and get the whole scoop. He'd take his camera along and take pictures in the park of the site where the campers went missing.

He was planning to make this, one of those sensationalist stories. An article, cleverly written, and including some of the legends of the loup-garou, would give the readers something fantastic to speculate on. It sounded like a goofy story angle, sure, but people were into that kind of thing these days, and he needed to sell a story. At any rate, it would be a pleasant day trip, and it would make him feel like he was actually doing something in his chosen profession.

And besides, he thought ruefully, if he didn't give his mom some money for his rent soon, she'd probably send him packing.

So he'd made a date with Gretchy for lunch at the Senator's Inn and asked her to see if she couldn't get her friend to join them. But, if the friend couldn't make it, well, he'd enjoy the time with Gretchy and get more details from her about the prints.

As expected, he got to the Ottawa city limits at 11:03. Thank goodness for GPS, because the city was confusing. He was eventually able to find the restaurant without too much difficulty though, and he finally found a parking spot. He went inside the Senator's Inn and glanced around. It was a swanky place, a vision of glass and metal: very modern. He could see that the stylish restaurant was already mostly full, obviously a popular spot for the downtown crowd. But it took only a moment for him to pick out Gretchy, sleek and attractive as ever. His friend had secured a table near the front so she could keep an eye out for Frank. Clever girl.

With one glance, he could tell she was doing well. He felt a twinge of jealousy. She was dressed in a smart navy blue suit with a pale pink shirt. It looked like silk. Nice. She'd cut her blond hair in a short bob, which made her look all business, but she was still as slim and attractive as he'd remembered.

What caught his attention, however, was the woman sitting next to Gretchy. Now, *that* was an attractive woman. He assumed this 'vision' must be Marielle Charbonneau, the owner of the cottage. But, whoever she was, he couldn't wait to meet her. This was going to be a very pleasant outing indeed, he mused.

He approached the table and acknowledged the two women. "Good morning, Gretchy. It's been too long." He stretched out his hand in greeting.

"Frank. On time as usual." Gretchy took his hand, then indicated the stunning woman sitting next to her. "This is Marielle Charbonneau, the woman I told you about. ... Marielle, I'd like you to meet Frank Barrett. We went to school together at Syracuse. We had some good times then, hey, Frank?" She slid him a conspiratorial look. "And now, I understand, he's writing a book or something."

Marielle lifted her hand toward Frank, as he winced at Gretchy's comment. Looking him directly in the eye, she spoke in a haughty air, with a low and melodic voice. "Nice to meet you, Frank." There was the hint of a French Canadian accent.

The woman was of indeterminate age, he'd judged. She was probably older than him, maybe early thirties. But did that really matter? A little experience was a good thing. She had magnificent wavy brown hair, charmingly streaked with premature gray, her eyes were large and soft, and she had a lithe athletic figure, undisguised beneath her tight black jeans and white blouse.

Frank knew he wasn't bad looking, himself, or socially inept. He could usually be discriminating in his choice of women, with his dark swarthy features and healthy physique. But he supposed that this suave and confident woman just might be out of his league. He felt a little overwhelmed by Marielle; there was something intimidating about her, like she came from old money and high society. And there was something slightly scary, too, a little dangerous and edgy. It gave him a thrill. Having lunch with this lovely creature would be most enjoyable, and challenging. Unwilling to break eye contact, Frank sat in the chair opposite Marielle, completely enthralled by her.

The waitress came over and took their order, and the three of them continued their polite conversation. They spoke of the fine weather, the advantages of living in the city, and how much they were enjoying their respective lunches. But time was passing, and, as much as he was enjoying the mundane conversation, Frank got down to the reason for their meeting. Turning to Marielle, he broached the subject, he thought, they had all come here to discuss.

"So, Gretchy tells me you own a cottage up on Lac-Belle, just north of the Gatineau Park. She said you found strange paw marks in the ground up there."

Marielle gave a lop-sided smirk and glanced side-long at Gretchy. "I thought your friend was here to take pictures of the park, Gretchy, and that you just wanted me to tell him about the area." Marielle shook her head at her friend in a disapproving manner and glanced back at Frank. "That was your friend, here, who spotted them. I had an outing at my place. I had asked her, and a couple of other friends of mine, to join me at the cabin for a barbecue last week."

Gretchy interrupted, all excited, "Yes, and a little way down the shore I saw them in the sand. Then, I followed them off into the woods. They were absolutely ... huge! So I called the others over to come see. Isn't that right, Marielle?"

"I suppose." Marielle looked bored. "They didn't look like much to me."

Gretchy smiled at Marielle. "Frank wants to write an article about the paw prints, do a story on the legend of the loup-garou; then connect it to the incident at the Gatineau Park. Did you know, one of those people who went missing from the park was an off-Broadway actor: almost famous? His story is sure to be picked-up by the AP." She was carrying on as if Marielle should find all of this a wonderful surprise. "Just think. This story could be read by thousands of people worldwide."

Marielle frowned, and then, inexplicably, her expression changed to interest. "So you think other people will be curious about those prints?"

She placed her hand on Frank's arm, and the contact was warm and electric. Frank felt an immediate connection. He could see a sparkle in her eyes; her smile was slight, but sensual. Perhaps he might have a chance with her, after all. His confidence returning, he gave her a smile of his own.

"I certainly hope so," Frank said. "I want to sell my article, after all."

The women both chuckled at his remark, and then Gretchy went on about the prints in great detail, while Frank jotted down notes. Marielle had little to say about the prints. She seemed uninterested in what Gretchy had to say. But she did seem interested in Frank. She kept giving him, what he thought, was meaningful looks, as they continued to chat over lunch.

The subject gradually changed from the paw prints to the latest news about the disappearance at the park, and then somehow managed to morph into a discussion of local politics, as Frank was still, somewhat, interested in that subject. Finally, they talked about what was new on television, and then lunch was over, and it was time to leave. Out in the parking lot, hugs were shared between Frank and Gretchy, as Marielle took her leave with a wave of her hand and one more smile for Frank.

"I really like that one, Gretchy. Can you give me her number?" He was not looking at his friend as he spoke. He was watching the sylphlike form of Marielle disappearing around the corner.

"I knew you'd like her. She's interesting, yes?" Gretchy watched Frank's smitten look with amusement. "She seems to like you, too, Frank. I'll see that you get her number. I'll call you tomorrow, but I have to get going now."

They parted, as old friends do, with promises that they would get together again soon, and then Gretchy was off to do some errands, while Frank was off to the park to take pictures.

⌒〜⌒

He found his way to the main parking area at Gatineau Park and was just getting out of his car, when Marielle's Audi pulled up next to him. It was strange to see her here in the park. He was surprised and confused. It could be a coincidence, but he thought that, maybe, she was following him. Well, this was interesting. He didn't think he had made *that* much of an impression on her.

She gracefully exited her car, and effortlessly strolled over toward him. She moved with a sexy animal grace. "Are you heading right back to Watertown after you take your pictures, Frank?"

"I ... ah." He was momentarily at a loss for words. Then he smiled. Suddenly, he was feeling very lucky. "No. ... What have you got in mind?"

"Well, if you've got a couple of hours, I could take you to my cottage. It's only a little way north of here, and it's still early. I think the tracks are still visible if you'd like to have a look."

He couldn't think of a better way to spend his afternoon than in the company of this fine woman. Even if the prints were gone by now, the trip would give him a chance to spend some time with her, get to know her. That seemed to be worth two—or even three—hours of his life. He decided to take her up on the offer.

Immediately. He could always take pictures at the Gatineau Park some other day.

"Sounds great," he said, trying not to smirk. "Let me just get my camera."

⁓⁂⁓

It was an altogether pleasant drive going north on 5 out of the park. The sun continued to shine, the traffic soon thinned out, and the conversation remained congenial. Frank was liking Marielle, more and more. Not only was she stunningly attractive, but, as it turned out, she also had a great sense of humor. And she seemed to know a lot about a great many subjects without coming off as a know-it-all. The best part: she genuinely seemed to like him. And, every now-and-then, she slid him a glance that, he felt, was hot and promising.

They talked about the area where her cottage was located: a lovely, out-of-the-way spot, surrounded by forest, but with a wonderful view of the lake. She added, that the fishing was superb, and the hunting in the area couldn't be beat. In fact, she told him, her cottage was originally built as a hunting cabin. She had enlarged it lately because she liked to party and wished to accommodate her friends. Now, she had two guest rooms so her friends could come up for a day of sport or leisure at the lake; then they could enjoy a cook-out and a campfire, possibly with some drinking, and they could stay overnight instead of driving home.

Frank started to wonder if, maybe, she had more in mind than just showing him some tracks in the mud, with the mention of guests staying over. And it was all right with him. If she offered to make a day of this excursion, he was certainly willing. A day, and possibly a night? Delightful.

They turned right, off of the Route Principale, and headed down Chemin Wells. Trees were thick on both sides, opening, only every now-and-then, to offer a sparse view of Lac-Belle or one of the very large country homes that sat along the shore. Then, after several minutes, they again turned to the right, down a street with no name. Immediately, the scene turned more rustic; this was not a densely populated area. It was practically wilderness, and it made him feel like he was going back in time to when the first adventurers had blazed their trails through the forests of Canada. It was incredibly beautiful, yet frightening in some indescribable way. Perhaps the utter remoteness of it. The sense of isolation.

Eventually, there was a break in the trees, and he could see a lovely cabin up ahead perched on the slope of a gentle hill that swept down toward a small open shoreline. The view of the lake was spectacular. The green of the trees around the edges of the lake were reflected in the still water, as well as the white fluffy clouds that drifted sleepily across the sky.

"Wow, Marielle, this is gorgeous. What a beautiful property, and no other houses around."

He was in total awe. This place was 'money'. It occurred to him, just then, that after an hour's worth of conversation—not to mention the time spent at lunch—he'd never found out just what Marielle did for a living. What kind of a reporter was he anyway? It was his job to glean information.

"Actually, this isn't Lac-Belle. It's a private lake that my family has owned for generations. But, come. ... Wait 'till you see the inside. You're going to love it," she purred and, coming around to his side of the car, she took his hand to lead him toward the cottage, a large and rustic structure that certainly looked inviting.

She had an uncanny way of distracting his thoughts, as he pictured himself in front of a fire with Marielle curled up in his arms, and he wanted to follow her inside, but ...

"Wait. Before we go into the cottage and get comfortable, I'd like to see those tracks. The light is good right now."

A look of intense disappointment shadowed Marielle's face. She seemed defeated, as though she had secretly hoped for a different occupation for the afternoon. "I think we would have a better time swimming, or ... but all right," she said with a sigh. "I think it was down here, where Gretchy first spotted the tracts in the sand, near the edge of the water."

She took his hand, and they strolled down to the water's edge, then along the shore for a couple of hundred feet. He searched the sand for indications of paw prints, but, not finding any tracks, his eyes kept drifting up to gaze out over the lake. It was so tranquil and lovely. "I could stay here forever," he said in an awed whisper.

He looked over at Marielle, and she was smiling at him in a peculiar way. "It was right over here that Gretchy wandered up into the woods," she said.

He nodded his acknowledgment, and, letting go of her hand, Frank followed a trail up into the woods. Marielle stayed on the shoreline waiting for him.

"I've found them," he shouted out from the woods. "My God, they're enormous! Come look."

"I've seen them already," she said with a sigh. "Actually, they're all over the place up here."

She made no effort to come into the woods to have a look. Patiently, she waited for him to emerge from the path entrance.

She could hear him moving behind the trees before she actually saw him sprinting out of the woods.

"This is going to be a great story. I have to get my camera," he said in an excited voice.

She called back to him, "And you think this story will be read by a lot of people?"

He had a beaming smile on his face as he headed back toward her. "With a few pictures of these prints, and the story of the loup-garou, it can't miss. It will be huge!"

"That's too bad," she whispered to herself. "I can't have that."

She moved to approach him. As she walked, slow and sure, she looked directly at him. With determination and a sad smile, she unbuttoned her blouse. Then, sliding her jeans down over her hips, she casually stepped out of them.

Frank stopped running and gazed at Marielle with surprise, and then delight. Apparently, she *must* have had another agenda, he mused. Did she feel as sexually aroused as he did? Could she possibly be as hot for him as he was for her? He could feel his excitement rising. They moved toward each other, him with wonder, her with incredible sexual grace. And as she continued to undress, he did the same. My God, this woman was beautiful, he thought, as she approached, unashamed and naked. Her eyes shone with lust and hunger, and he felt their power deep inside.

Wow, this *was* going to be a very profitable and enjoyable trip, after all, the start of a great story, both on the page, and in the sheets. He was thinking that he must be the luckiest man in the world. Right up until, ...

... she turned into a wolf.

HE COMES IN THE NIGHT

Agnes rolled over in her sleep and groaned. She realized the ache in her hip was excruciating and wasn't going to go away. Dang it all. She might as well get up. She didn't really want to. She wanted to roll over again and go back to sleep, slip back into the dream she was having and forget about everything else, but the damn pain always got in the way of her sleep.

Slowly, she raised herself up on one elbow and reached over to her nightstand, groping for her bifocals. This movement caused pain to radiate down her arm. *Great, a new pain to go along with the one in my hip,* she thought. Life was becoming a series of pains and discomforts, indigestion and neuralgia, dizziness and forgetfulness. It was becoming a series of days that were all the same, except for the location of her latest ache.

She put her glasses on and looked around, slightly confused. Then, after a moment, she recognized the small room that she occupied at the Worther Nursing Home, her easy chair in the corner, her desk and television in the opposite corner, the picture of her long dead husband on the wall.

She glanced at the clock. Huh, it was after ten. She must have slept through breakfast. The nurse's aides who manned the night shift were supposed to see to it that everyone ate their breakfast and took their morning pills before the end of their shift. But with their usual diligence, they totally had forgotten all about her. Or they had figured that, if she wanted to sleep, why bother with her. One less mouth to feed ... literally.

She was too groggy to call for breakfast now. She wasn't hungry anyway. The food around here didn't taste very good to her. She had lost quite a bit of her sense of taste the last few years. But instead of being able to eat *anything,* since the taste of the food shouldn't bother her, she usually wanted to eat *nothing,* because she no longer found any joy in eating.

She swung her legs over the side of her bed and a wave of dizziness swept over her. She clung to the bed rail. She knew she should wait a minute before trying to get up, but she had to pee. ... And she had to pee, now. She thought about calling for the aide, since the one who would respond at this hour was Cherie, one of the day girls, a very nice girl, whom she liked a lot, but she hated to bother anyone. And she really thought she would be fine as soon as she stood.

She was just about to put her strength to the test, when Cherie gave a light rap on the door and peeked her pert blond head inside to see if Agnes was still sleeping.

"Oh, good, you're up. Sally was worried about you, since you didn't want to get up when she came around to see if you needed help getting to breakfast."

Cherie was all smiles, like she was every day. She was a person who really cared. You could see it in her warm brown eyes, and she had the nicest manner, such a sweet girl. Not like that Sally. Sally was always stern and grumpy faced. *Sally worry about her? Not a chance.*

"You still look a little sleepy. Do you need help getting to the bathroom?" Cherie came over to the bedside and slipped a hand beneath Agnes's arm. Agnes would have objected—she wasn't *that* infirm yet—but since it was Cherie, she let the girl give her a hand walking to the bathroom. As she moved, she realized just how dizzy she was, and she leaned on Cherie, as she watched the room swim around her. Flashes of light danced behind her eyes.

Cherie helped her to get situated and then left her alone with some privacy to take care of her business. After she relieved herself, Agnes stood at the sink washing her hands. She looked at herself in the mirror and saw the same old disappointing face that greeted her every morning. At ninety-two, her hair, what little she had left, was as white as her bathroom walls, and her face was warn with age. It made her feel tired just to look at herself.

But, ... wait. Something about her face was different this morning. There was something new and unusual. On the left side of her neck were two, tiny, red, round holes. She leaned in closer to have a better look. Yes, there they were. She remembered the dream she was having just moments ago, and she wondered if there could be a connection. She had been dreaming of Prince Alexander, after all.

A knowing smile alighted on her lips as she reminisced about the events her imagination had laid out for her in her sleep. She hadn't had a dream about him for a very long time, not since she was a young girl. And, now—come to think of it—when she had dreamed of him then, these same markings had shown up on her neck in the morning.

"He must be a vampire," she chuckled to herself. Suddenly, the day seemed a little brighter. She hadn't had an erotic dream in ages. She felt her face flush like a schoolgirl. Guess she wasn't as old as she had thought, after all. She called to Cherie when she was done, and the young aide came in and helped her back to the side of her bed.

"Are you feeling up for some breakfast, Agnes? Will you need a wheelchair?"

An impish grin had found its way onto Agnes's face, and she had a definite twinkle in her eye. "I think that sounds wonderful. I suddenly have an appetite. But I won't need the wheelchair. If you would come along with me—just to be safe—I think I'll be able to walk to the dining room."

With that, she took Cherie's arm and headed off down the hall, not exactly dancing, but there was, at least, a new spring in her step. Life had taken a turn for the interesting, she thought. Maybe, she'd even go to the community movie this evening. Maybe, she'd have a conversation with some of the other 'inmates'. Maybe, she'd stay up late. Today she was feeling very social and, certainly, less grumpy. Life was still good.

But right after dinner her exuberance for life had waned. Long before the evening movie could get underway, Agnes was, again, feeling the weight of her ailments, the depression of her surroundings, and a very strong insistent urge to sleep. She retired early that evening for the twelfth time in two weeks.

After checking the daily itinerary, as she did every morning, Cherie popped in to see how her friend Agnes was doing. She was afraid she would find her still abed, since Agnes had been sleeping more and more all the time. It seriously worried Cherie. She had grown quite found of the old lady, and she tried to spend extra time with her. Cherie knew that Agnes never had any visitors. She had no friends on the outside, no relatives left to care about her. Cherie didn't like to see anybody be that lonely or abandoned. *Well, I care about you, Agnes,* she would tell herself, and she meant it.

She was pleased to see that Agnes was up. But one look at the old one's face told her she was probably not doing well. Her face was drawn and listless, and her skin had an ugly pallor. She was getting so thin and frail, she looked like the wind could blow her away if ever a fresh breeze found its way down these stagnant corridors. And still, Agnes greeted her with a smile.

"How are you feeling today, honey?" Cherie said, as she sat down on the bed next to Agnes.

"I'm feeling good, Cherie." The old lady patted her hand. "Very happy today. I had the most wonderful dream last night. It was so good, I almost hated to get up this morning."

"Well, I'm glad you did. I'd have to talk to myself this morning if you were still asleep," Cherie teased. "Shall we walk down to breakfast now?"

"I think you had better get the wheelchair for me this morning, hon. I don't think I'm spry enough today to walk to the dining room."

"You just sit right there, and I'll be back in a jiff." Cherie patted her knee and left to go fetch a wheelchair. She wiped a tear away from the corner of her eye as a moment of regret pressed down on her heart. She was afraid her friend Agnes was on a chronic downward spiral. She felt her throat tighten, as she forcefully put a pleasant smile on her face.

※

The distance across the grand entry hall in the large Chateau du Mort was only perhaps thirty feet, and yet, it felt to Aggie that it took simply forever for Prince Alexander to cross the space.

"I've missed you so, my darling," she purred as he approached. "You know every minute away from you is torture."

The prince moved with a grace that was preternatural, so like his kind. His steps were those of a young and healthy animal, unhurried and sure. His sensual good looks stirred the imagination; his hair sleek and shiny as a panther; his eyes as dark and fathomless as the blackest night.

He reached for her and grabbed her around the waist, pulling her toward him in a hungry embrace. "I am glad that you are so welcoming, my Aggie. To resist me is, of course, pointless. When I want something, I take it. And, you, my dear, I want very much. It fills me with joy to know you want me as well. And so, I have decided, that it is time for me to claim you."

She was filled with hot desire. She could think of nothing she would want more than for him to claim her. She never wanted to leave his side.

He placed one of his hands on her hip and with the other, he took her hand in his and stretched it out. Her mind whorled as they began to dance. Music filled the air. In the corner of the room, a small orchestra was playing a waltz. She threw her head back and watched the intricate shapes in the molded ceiling swirl in her vision, enjoying the dizzying feeling.

Suddenly, the music stopped, and the orchestra was gone. They were no longer dancing, yet her head was still spinning. "Oh, my. That was delightful," she said. "It is so wonderful when I'm here with you, my prince."

He smiled down at her with a knowing look. "Soon you will come back to me, sweet Aggie, and then you will never leave me again."

⁓⁓⁓

The hospital room, where Agnes lay, was a vision of antiseptic cleanliness. There was nothing extraneous inside the room, nothing to give the place a sense of personal charm. There were none of the small touches that had made Agnes's room at the home 'her room'. Here, at the hospital, it was anybody's room—and nobody's room.

A nurse was standing beside Agnes's bed looking over her chart. She glanced at the monitors on the wall by the head of the bed, and then made some notations on the chart. She looked over at Cherie as she realized someone else was in the room.

Cherie was still wearing her garb from the Worther Nursing Home, her name plate visible above her pocket, and the nurse mistook her for someone who worked at the hospital. "She's stable for the moment, but she's in an inevitable decline," she said, as if Cherie had asked her a question.

Sadly, Cherie looked at Agnes's sleeping features and noticed a hint of a smile lurking at the corner of her mouth. She came a little closer to the bed. "She looks happy at least."

"I'm afraid that is just involuntary muscle reflex. Her corotid artery is severely blocked. It's been shutting off blood to the brain for a while now. I doubt there is much cognition left. It's too late for a corotid endarterectomy, she's much too weak. Her age would preclude that option at any rate." Not realizing that Cherie was a friend, she added, "She would probably be better off dead. She's got no real quality of life now, no sense of existence. And, I understand, she has no family."

"Well, I think she looks happy."

Cherie stood over her friend, seeing the tube down her throat, seeing the IV in her arm, seeing the heart monitor pulse over her head, seeing her friend slip slowly into death. She couldn't stop a tear from forming in the corner of her eye. *I will miss you, Agnes,* she thought. She had come to say her last goodbye.

The nurse dropped the chart at the foot of the bed and headed toward the door. "Happy? Not very likely," she said in a voice she, obviously, thought was too low for Cherie to hear.

After the nurse left, Cherie sat on the edge of the bed, sadly watching the pale face of her friend with the enigmatic smile. And, gently, she took Agnes's hand in hers.

⁊ℽ

He came up to stand behind her as she finished her preparations for the ball, and he gently took her hand in his. She saw his handsome figure just to her right in the looking glass, his eyes gazing lovingly upon her. Then she looked at herself. She was particularly beautiful this evening, more beautiful than she had ever been. Her youthful carriage was strong and lean; her young skin was radiant; her hair was thick and glossy, piled in a chignon on top of her head. She was wearing a long beaded evening gown in the colors of the peacock. And, like a peacock, it shimmered with iridescence and grandeur.

Behind her, reflected in the glass, she could see her new opulent bedroom, also decorated in fabulous colors. It was incredibly large with a vaulted ceiling. Fine woodwork framed the walls, where magnificent paintings and tapestries hung in abundance. She had never experienced anything so fine, anything so magnificently grand. Prince Alexander must, indeed, be fabulously rich, she thought, and he wants to share it all with me.

"Are you ready, my Aggie?" he whispered softly and sensually in her ear. "All of my friends are waiting in the ball room below to meet you. They are all thrilled that you shall be joining us."

"Yes, I believe I am ready." She smiled at his reflection in the mirror. She felt immense love and tremendous joy, and she was filled with anticipation, as well. She couldn't wait to meet the hundreds of friends he had assembled for her introduction.

She sighed with the notion of how happy she was, and she leaned back to press lovingly against him, letting the encompassing warmth of his body radiate into hers. "Will you stay with me now, forever?"

"I am so glad that you decided to join us, my darling, my precious Aggie. It is my pleasure to be with you now." He slid his hand slowly down the length of her naked arm. "And I promise you, that I will be with you until the very end of your days." Then, leaning forward, he gently pressed his lips to the side of her neck.

She felt a little thrill of pain, and she closed her eyes and threw her head back. Then, suddenly, all pain and sorrow left her mind. And in its place, a radiant light filled her thoughts and soul, and she expired in her rapture. Dying in his arms.

DEALING WITH THE DEVIL

"Damn you," Dennis Rathmore growled through his clenched teeth, as he kicked his competition skateboard across the room. He heard a satisfying thump, as it landed on its side, up against the ugly utilitarian desk of his motel room. The sublimated graphic of a red devil, with horns, a tail, and a grinning face, seemed to mock him from the surface of his board, laughing at him; It was laughing at his pathetic performance.

He had just completed his third Ultimate Games, ending up a close fourth, and fourth didn't get him a medal. He had yet to win *any* medal. He knew he deserved one. He was good, good enough to take the gold, even. But every time he came close, he managed to screw it up somehow, and this time was no different. He had it going into the last round. The gold was his for the taking ... until he choked.

Dennis walked across the room and gave the grinning board another sound kick. "Screw you. I'm getting another board as soon as I get back to LA. You suck!"

Thump. Thump. He gave it another couple of kicks for good measure. Then, his anger ebbing, he stared at the board as his breathing slowed. He felt on the verge of tears now. Shit! He wasn't going to cry. Damn it! Abruptly, he turned his back and walked to the window, running his hand through his long blond curls. He stared out at the drab landscape, attempting to calm himself down.

He worked his ass off all year, and, just like last year, the prize was yanked away from him at the last minute. He couldn't take it. He hated his co-competitors, and he wished them nothing but ill. They didn't deserve those medals like he did.

His eyes narrowed as he pictured them missing a trick during the Vert Competition, falling from their boards at the tip of their biggest air jumps, and landing painfully on their heads. The thought gave him only a momentary pleasure. He blinked the satisfying thought out of his head and actually looked out the window.

The view looked like crap. There was an expanse of parking lot, a few nondescript vehicles parked there, some nondescript buildings in the distance, probably other motels. There were no lovely plantings of trees and flowers like they have down south. No, here in Cleveland, he figured, everything was probably required to be the same color by law. The view was all shades of gray and looked as bleak as he felt.

"Board Devil," he huffed in disgust. That was his nickname back in LA: 'Board Devil'. Maybe he should change it to 'board bedeviled'. He glanced over his left shoulder at his board lying impotently against the desk, and he spoke to the effigy of a devil smiling back at him from the board's surface. "If I could, I'd sell my soul to the Devil for the gold medal. I would, damn it. I'd sell my soul."

Dennis could feel the tear, he could no longer contain, roll slowly and humiliatingly down his cheek. He wiped it away quickly as a tentative knock sounded on the door. "Yeah, who is it?" He wiped more tears and nose dribble on his sleeve.

A deep voice said, "The room service you called for, Mr. Rathmore."

The voice was compelling, and the timbre hypnotic. Dennis wanted to tell, whoever it was, to go away, but instead he rose to answer the door, saying, "Just a minute." He opened the door and looked out. "Yes?"

On the other side of the door was a tall man dressed in black, incredibly good looking. He had slicked back, black hair and dark penetrating eyes. His smile was turned up at the corners of his mouth, showing incredibly white perfect teeth. His smile was not so much friendly, as wicked.

"You called." It wasn't a question.

"Did I?" Dennis felt confused. "What did I want?"

"It's my understanding you want a gold medal. Isn't that what you asked for?"

Dennis stared at this man like he had horns growing out of his head. "How do you know what I want? And who are you?"

"I," the strange man said, raising one eyebrow. "Am the Devil's advocate. I'm here to strike a deal with you. Isn't that what you wanted?"

Could this be for real? Dennis thought. *How else would he know what I just said?* And looking at this guy, wow, he was mesmerizing. Really. ... Who else could it be? "Strike a deal, huh? And what is the deal?"

The advocate invited himself in, moving with uncanny grace and seeming to fill up the entire room with dynamic presence. He shut the door and nodded. "We don't really want to do business in the hall, now, do we?" He pulled the chair out from the desk, with a surreptitious look at the skateboard, and invited Dennis to sit. The advocate remained standing. "I'm authorized to present you with the usual contract," he said, drawing Dennis in with a hypnotic gaze. "You get something that you want. In this case, you win the gold medal. And we get something that we want, namely, your soul. We will allow you to live out your natural life. We have, you see, all the time in the world. We won't take your life. We have no use for that. We just want sole possession of your soul after you die. So what do you say? Do we have a deal?"

Dennis didn't really give two shits about his soul. He didn't believe in Heaven anyway. And besides, they were talking about a long time in the future. He could promise his soul away, for now. He had the rest of his life to figure out how to get it back again if he wanted it. But what he really wanted, more than anything, was that gold medal. He'd said it to himself only a few minutes ago, 'I'd sell my soul for a gold medal', and he'd meant it.

"If I do this, when do I get my gold medal?"

"Your deal will include: you getting the very next gold medal for the Vert Skateboard Competition at next year's Ultimate Games. Is that soon enough for you?" The advocate's eyes twinkled. He knew he had this fish hooked on the line. He just needed to reel him in.

"OK," Dennis said. "I get the gold medal at the next Ultimate Games, or no deal."

"Fair enough." The advocate smiled as he pulled a contract, already drawn up, from his pocket and pushed it across the desk surface. "I'll even add, that we won't lay claim to your soul, unless you declare you are satisfied with the deal. Of course, if we come through with our end, you can't renege."

"Works for me," Dennis said, and he signed his name with a flourish across the bottom of the page.

A little less than one year later, Dennis Rathmore was once again ready to compete for the gold medal in the Vert Skateboard Competition. This time, the games were being held in San Antonio. He heard the city was beautiful, but again, all he could see from his motel room window was a large parking lot and the cars parked there. This time, however, he did not find the view bleak. The sun was shining bright and pretty, and, as far as he was concerned, the day couldn't be more pleasant.

He had not trained at all—not even a little—because he knew he had this one in the bag. No sense knocking yourself out practicing day and night like last year, when all he had to do was show up. He was almost feeling sorry for his competition. Those poor saps had busted their butts all year, and they all thought they would be the one to win. The thought made him laugh. He was really going to enjoy this.

He was just replaying his winning speech in his head, when a knock sounded on his door. A familiar hypnotic voice spoke through the door. "Mr. Rathmore, I have what you ordered."

Dennis was a little nervous about the advocate showing up before the competition, but he was unable to stop himself from answering the door. "What do you want? I haven't won the gold medal yet. My soul isn't yours until then."

The advocate stepped blithely into the room, holding a bottle in his left hand. "You'll need to drink this before you compete, or you won't be able to win the gold."

"Drink that, huh?" Dennis asked, taking the bottle from the advocate's hand and scrutinizing the blue contents. "What's in it?"

"It's a magic elixir. How did you think we were going to be able to grant your request if you didn't practice for the competition all year? I'm afraid we will have to enlist some dark magic. Don't worry, this drink will make you unbeatable, even if you did nothing but waste the past year. You'll take the gold, as per our agreement."

Dennis didn't want to drink the, so-called, magic elixir, but the advocate's voice was so persuasive, his eyes so intense, that he grabbed the bottle and downed the liquid in one swift move. "There, now be gone. I have to prepare for the competition."

The advocate gave him a knowing amused smirk. "By all means, prepare. So diligent you are. One has to admire your tireless work ethic," he said with disdain.

Dennis scowled back, squinting his eyes. This guy was a real pain in the ass. He wanted him out of his room immediately. "Get out!"

Without any further prompting, the advocate exited the motel room. There was no need to linger. "I'll be back after you collect your gold medal. I'd say good luck, but you won't need it."

The door closed quietly behind him.

⁓⁓

The motel room door swung open, and Dennis stumbled in, giddy as a school girl. He had been out celebrating his gold medal win for the last six hours, and he was slightly inebriated. Well, maybe a little more than slightly. But he deserved it; he deserved this glory, and everyone's admiration.

He'd be famous now, maybe get an advertising endorsement. Walking across the motel room, he smiled to himself. He remembered the competition that afternoon with glee. Not only did he win the gold, but he performed tricks even he could not have imagined. And the air he got with his jumps, why, it was nothing less than spectacular. They were even going to put his name on one of the tricks he'd performed: the Rathmore move. His name would always be remembered; he would go down in history.

Wow, the Devil really did come through. But, he reflected, all sure of himself, the Devil left a glaring gap in that contract. Dennis chuckled to himself at his own brilliance. According to the agreement, unless Dennis was satisfied with the outcome, the Devil would have no claim on his soul. And, of course, Dennis didn't intend to ever admit that he got his end of the bargain. Oh, no. He'd have his gold medal and his soul too. Dennis threw himself on the bed and laughed until he could laugh no more, until there was a knock on the door.

Dennis was waiting for this moment. He would relish it. Just wait until the Devil finds out that I've outsmarted him. *Outsmarted the Devil,* he thought. *I deserve another gold medal for that, too.* He jumped up happily from the bed and threw open the door.

As expected, the Devil's advocate was standing on the other side. "Well?" he asked. "And how are you enjoying your gold medal? Are you satisfied with the outcome?"

Dennis snickered at the advocate. He believed he was holding all the cards. As far as he was concerned, the advocate could 'go to hell'. "Well, to tell you the truth, I'm not satisfied. Oh, no. I think I deserve to win the gold for the next six years in a row. I need to set a record, you see. Only then can I truly be happy. And you did say that I *had* to be satisfied with the deal, did you not?"

"This is highly irregular," said the advocate. "We do not renegotiate. You agreed to sell your soul for one gold medal, which is now in your possession. Now agree that we have held up our end of the bargain or face the consequences."

"You can't scare me. You're all bluster. You know I've caught you in a loophole. Now you either agree to my renegotiation, or you can just leave, and I keep the gold medal and my soul." There was a very ugly look of smugness on Dennis's face. He'd have a promise for six gold medals in short order.

"I see." A slight disappointed frown appeared between the advocate's eyes. "Very well. I'll take your ultimatum to my superiors." And, with that said, the advocate disappeared. He didn't even bother to exit through the door.

Dennis sauntered back over to the bed and was about to lie down, when there came another knock to his door. "Thought you'd change your mind," he said. "Didn't take you long, either, did it?"

He opened the door to find several officials and a nurse with a syringe. The official spoke up, "We need to take a sample of your blood and urine, Mr. Rathmore. It's time for your drug tests. Just routine."

Dennis was confused. There had never been any drug testing required for the Ultimate Games before. He didn't get it. "When did this start?" he asked.

"New this year," the official said. "It was all spelled out in your application." The nurse started to prepare her stuff on the desk.

He hadn't even read the application. He'd been a participant in the Ultimate Games for four years now. The last three games had had no drug testing. This was new. Damn. He should have read the thing before he signed it. Too late now. He had to comply, whether he liked it or not. With a growing ache in his gut, he worried just what was in that elixir the Devil's advocate had given him?

Three days later, Dennis was disqualified, and he was stripped of his medal. He was humiliated and discredited. He was also barred from any further competition in the Ultimate Games. There would be no glory for him. There would be no advertising contracts. They had even removed his name form his best trick. Now, the view out his motel room window was more than bleak. His life was in the toilet. It was over. He was left with his soul ... but big deal.

"What good is my stinking soul," he cried. "I'd sell it right now to get my good name back."

There was a light tapping on his door, and Dennis was all too happy to answer it. In the hallway stood the advocate, dark and interesting as ever. Dennis noticed a paper and pen in his hand. "May I come in?" he asked politely.

A defeated Dennis waved him in with a hand. "They never had drug testing before," he murmured.

"Well," said the advocate. "The Devil *is* in the details they say."

"OK, I'm ready to deal," Dennis whimpered.

"Indeed you are. But, this time, the deal is different. We will give you your good name back. You will be cleared of all wrong doing, and you will reclaim the gold medal—only one—no more. But …" The advocate hesitated. This was *his* time to enjoy the moment. "As soon as you are cleared, we will immediately claim your soul. And, this time, your life shall go with it."

Dennis felt there was no real life left for him without his reputation. He didn't care about anything else. He wanted his name to live on in glory. He couldn't stomach leaving this life as a failure. He wanted to be remembered as a 'somebody'. He couldn't die a 'nobody'.

The advocate waited for Dennis's mind to stop churning, and then he prompted, "That's the deal. Take it, or leave it."

Sadly, but with resolve, Dennis took the paper and the pen from the advocate's hand, and, signing his name, he declared reluctantly, "I'll take it."

BON APPETIT

He sat down at the keyboard of his old computer. It had been so long since he'd written anything it almost seemed unfamiliar to him, like it was some stranger you meet somewhere, who thinks he knows you, but you don't recall his name; then, suddenly, you do. He had been meaning to enter another recipe on his food blog for days now, but he just hadn't found the time. He couldn't seem to dig himself out of the deep hole he'd found himself in lately. He was in a perpetual funk. His life was not going at all the way he had planned. And sometimes it felt like he was actually falling apart, losing important pieces of himself every day. That's why he felt he had to get back on track; he had to try to get back to his old life and his old interests, before everything disintegrated for good.

With an effort, he brought his mind back to the computer screen and tried to concentrate. What should today's food item be? He thought for a minute and imagined what dish he might like to eat right now. A longing for cervella came into his mind, and, at that thought, his mouth began to water. He couldn't recall seeing any articles written on that particular delicacy for quite some time, so he figured his entry would be, kind of, unique. He closed his eyes and imagined the cervella fritte, or fried brains, laid out before him. Yum. It was making him hungry.

He typed in a title to his entry, Cervella: How to find them and what kind to look for. That was a good start. His fingers flew over the keyboard as his excitement for the subject grew. He talked about the best markets, where you would find the largest selection. He talked about the little out-of-the-way places that might offer something special. He talked about selecting only the best, most tender, and succulent cuts. And he advised to always try to get the youngest cervella you can find. The younger the tissue, the less it has been used by the animal, he added, and the fresher it will taste. Like any other meat, it gets tough from use.

As to the proper way to eat them? Well, he would definitely have to recommend they be eaten raw. Oh, and a little red sauce on the side was, of course, always nice. And for the presentation, a natural bowl will suffice. No need to get too fancy. You want to concentrate on the taste, not on how well dressed it might be.

He typed a few more lines, but, eventually, his mind fogged up again. Already, he was becoming bored by his own blog, and, in truth, writing about this marvelous food was making him hungry. He realized, just then, that he hadn't eaten anything all day.

Well, I'll just have to do something about that, he reasoned. And what better thing could he have to eat, than the very dish he had been writing about in his blog?

Determined to go out and find this tantalizing treat, he dragged himself to the door, and, with the effort of his blind hunger, he opened it, intending to go out and search for the thing he so craved. The air was cold and damp with a slight drizzle, but he didn't mind this. The weather never seemed to bother him.

Stepping out the door, he glanced across the street and saw some of his old gang approaching. Apparently, they too had dug themselves out of their own respective holes to come join him for his evening repast. Well, and why not? He thought. There was plenty for all. It was going to be a jolly good party, as soon as they hooked up with some delicious young women.

He fell in with this familiar crowd, and, exchanging desperate looks that said, 'let's go get some food', they all dragged themselves down the street, moving together as if obsessed. They had one thought on their minds. One thought shared among them:

"Brains! Brains! Brains!"

They said it in chorus, as they headed downtown for a light supper of human brains, maybe served in a fine red sauce. Then, afterword, their appetite appeased, they would all drag their rotting bodies back into their respective holes until it was time for them to feed again.

STRANGE AND DISTURBING

A HUNTING
WE WILL GO

Only a little way further through the woods, he knew the trees would open upon a fine meadow where he could count on being alone, because it was isolated from the nearest village by about a ten mile drive, and then a long hike from the road. In this meadow, he had a wide field of vision, and he could get a good clean shot. And the deer came often, confident that man would not find them this far out in the wilderness.

So far today, Mike hadn't had any luck at his other favorite hunting spots. But here, he knew, he could usually count on a kill. It was a damn good place to hunt. And if he didn't see any deer at this site, he figured, well then, that meant they just weren't out anywhere today. He tried to keep his mind on the hunt, but ever since he left home this morning he had been pestered with annoying and restless thoughts. He couldn't seem to shut his brain off for even a couple of minutes and just relax. Hunting usually did

STRANGE AND DISTURBING

the trick for him when he was stressed, but today, his thoughts were so turbulent, he doubted he could find peace, even in the quiet of nature and the manly satisfaction of bagging a deer.

Without his willing it, the little 'disturbance' in his thoughts came nudging back into his brain, unwilling to be silent, begging for his attention. He had to acknowledge it. The damn thing wouldn't leave him alone. Yesterday evening he had broken it off with his long-time girlfriend Chloe. And the memory of this ugly scene was making him angry. It wasn't that he didn't like her anymore. It wasn't that she wasn't attractive. He couldn't even say he had gotten bored. No, the only reason he had called it quits, was because his wife was starting to get suspicious. He knew that if Grace found out, his whole life would be ruined.

Now, his wife, Grace, was not the vindictive type. She would create no ugly scene, no yelling, no recriminations, but she positively would not stand for it. She'd divorce him in a second, and his house and home would be gone. That was a fact. He felt he loved his wife. He truly did. And believed they shared a history that made his life full. After all, she was the best companion a man could ask for. She liked the same things as him, and understood him and his ambitions as no one else had. They even had the same political opinions. And, he also had to admit, they had a great sex life together, even if she was starting to show her age. But, most importantly—and a sad fact of life it was too—she was his boss's daughter and losing her would cause his whole life to come crashing down.

He took his orange hat off and ran his hand through, what was left of his brown and gray hair, and wiped the sweat from his forehead. The day wasn't that hot, but it had been a long walk. And, at fifty-one, he wasn't as fit as he used to be.

It just seemed a shame to have to break Chloe's heart. She was the true victim here. She didn't deserve the treatment she was getting. He couldn't blot out of his mind the picture of her tear-filled face, and her pleading voice asking him, "Why? Why? Don't you love me anymore?"

Mike had to gulp down a pesky piece of phlegm that crept up into his throat, choking him. Must be a high pollen count today. Chloe really seemed to care for him, love him even. She always looked at him with a tender smile, laughed at his jokes, stared lovingly into his eyes. As far as she was concerned, he could do no wrong. Right up until yesterday, that is. And she was the best of them all, he had to admit: the best one he'd ever had.

Not like Fran. At the thought of Fran the hunk of phlegm found its way down his throat and into his gut, making him queasy. It had been humiliating when he found out that Fran was only using him to get a better position at the factory. He could feel his lip curl in distaste. What a bitch she was. ... Well, she was old history. Live and learn, as they say.

Now, Mary, he recalled fondly, was in it for the sex. What a hot one she was. The thought of Mary, splayed out on the bed before him, gave him a moment of pleasure. He tried to keep his mind on memories of Mary. They were all good, and they made him smile. But his little 'disturbance' came budging back into his brain again like some gremlin from hell, haunting him. This made him angry again, and it was fucking up his hunting trip.

Who the hell was he angry with, anyway? He wondered. He couldn't be angry at Chloe. She wasn't the one that wanted to break up. She'd always been there for him. Canceling any other appointments—canceling her life—to devote time for him. He could always count on Chloe. ... No, it wasn't Chloe.

His wife? Again, here was a loving woman. She'd backed him for years, through thick and thin, even when her father disapproved of him at first. She had always been his strong supporter. He had to admit that, even if her divorcing him would ruin everything he worked for, he couldn't really blame her. He knew what her reaction might be if she ever found out about his women. He knew that all along.

But, God damn it! A man has needs! Even if he does get great sex at home, isn't he entitled to some variety? Wasn't it in a man's nature to hunt down and dominate the female? He couldn't be expected to go against his own nature, could he?

Suddenly he felt indignant. What more could anyone ask of him, anyway? He'd done the noble thing and given up Chloe, didn't he? He did this for his wife, a grand magnanimous gesture. He should be the hero here. But something niggled at his brain. He couldn't quite put his finger on it, but it made him angry. A hint of conscience, perhaps? He determinedly brushed the feeling away.

A man has needs.

Finally, he broke through into the clearing, without really having registered the last few steps of his trek. Well, he was here now. Time to get serious and do some hunting. Scoping out the meadow for any sign of deer, a movement to his right, and about two hundred yards away, caught his eye. It was a hand waving above a florescent orange jacket. Damn. Another hunter was already here. He didn't want to accidentally get shot, so he waved his hand in acknowledgment.

He was thinking about what other hunting spot he might try next, since this one was apparently occupied, when the other hunter started to move in his direction. Oh, great, he thought. That was just what he needed right now, a social hunter. Good grief, he better get out of here before he was dragged into some inane conversation with this backwoods yahoo.

But before he could turn and make his escape, a light melodic voice called out through the meadow. "Hey, hold up there," the voice chimed. It was definitely female and sounded like slow moving cigarette smoke drifting across a dim barroom. Mike stopped in his tracks. He just had to see the body that was attached to that sultry voice. He waited with interest as she drew closer.

She carefully stepped through the tall grass, moving like a gazelle through the African plain. A few more swishing steps and she was close enough for him to see her clearly. She removed her hat with a swing of her head, and a cascade of brilliant auburn burned on his retinas.

She was indeed as lovely as her voice: a true beauty. How nice to come upon this vision out here in the woods, far away from prying eyes. He was beginning to feel very lucky. Screw the deer, he thought. This hunting trip was already a success. "I've never seen you out here before. ... Been hunting long?" Mike asked. He could feel his old pick-up mode kicking in.

"Do you mean just today, or in general?" Her words slipped through her lips like something wet and sweet.

"Either one." Mike couldn't keep his face from betraying him. He gave her a cocky smirk.

"Well," she said, stretching luxuriously. "I've been here since early this morning, and I've had no luck, what-so-ever ... until now."

Mike decided to take that remark 'until now' as a compliment. Well, he mused, it's your lucky day *now*, baby. But aloud, he said, "I've been hunting this spot for years."

"Oh, I'm sorry. Am I encroaching? I guess I'll be the one who moves on."

"No, no, no, you stay right where you are. I've been hunting this spot for years, true, but I have to admit, I've never seen anything like you out here before."

She put her finger to the corner of her lip, considering him. Then she tilted her head to the side and smiled, a slow sensual smile. "What's your name, hunter? I'm Desirae."

Mike felt confident. There was no denying that smoldering look in her eyes. This woman was hot for him, he could tell. Perhaps it was the setting, earthy and isolated, a chance meeting in the wild, that made him want to throw caution to the wind. He was definitely turned on and he knew, by his natural instinct in women, that she was turned on, too. "I'm Mike Stringom," he said, as he held his hand out, in what seemed, a friendly gesture. But as their hands clasped, he pulled her into his arms and planted his hungry lips on hers.

His instincts were correct, as usual, he thought with smug satisfaction, as she melted into his arms, throwing one arm around his shoulders, while holding her gun with the other. The kiss was long and intense. Their tongues explored each other's mouths. They pressed their bodies close, until the pressure of their clothes became restricting. His hands went deftly to the buttons of her jacket, eventually sliding it down off her shoulders and onto the grass below.

She pulled away reluctantly, and their lips parted. "Excuse me, Mike," she said as she moved farther away from him. "I need to take care of something." Then she casually threw him a promising smile over her shoulder, and she walked a short distance to some tall concealing grass.

Women, Mike thought, they always had to take care of something before getting to it. No problem. He could wait. But not for too long.

"Mike?" The voice floated up from out of the grass.

"Huh?" he answered.

"Your wife told me you were a philanderer. She was certainly right."

Mike's brow frowned in bewilderment. This woman mentioning his wife was definitely out of place. It felt vaguely like an invasion of his privacy, and his hackles rose. "My wife?" he asked in consternation.

"Yes, she told me all about you, but I had to make sure it was you, of course," she said, as though her remark was an obvious statement. "Before I could complete my contract."

Mike turned to her with a look of surprise and disbelief. He didn't hear the sound of her gun. He didn't have time to figure it all out. He was dead before the sound could reach him. He was dead before he hit the ground.

The huntress walked casually over to examine her kill. Yes. He was definitely dead, a clean shot right between the eyes. She removed a small zip bag from one of her vest pockets and squatted down beside the body.

It was a shame really, she thought. He was such a handsome man, and a great kisser too. But she really felt no regret in killing him. She rarely felt much of anything at all. To her, Mike's dead body equaled big money. And she had many things she wanted to buy with it.

She took out a small knife from another of her half dozen pockets, and cutting off a small piece of poor Mike, she put it in the zip bag: a little trophy for herself.

"No hard feelings, Mike," she said, though he could no longer hear her. "But a girl has needs." And with no regrets, she walked off into the woods.

I THINK, THEREFORE, I AM

The man in the lab coat was unremarkable. He was of average height, average weight, average face. His hair was a medium brown and so were his eyes. He was wearing glasses, the common sort. His face looked pretty much like everybody you pass on the street and promptly forget. The only thing that made him stand out—if anything did—was the curious glint in his eye. A spark of intelligence, perhaps. A spark of something.

He crossed a room that was definitely a laboratory, of some kind, and stopped in front of a console with an unusual array of switches, lights and knobs. There was a display panel with interesting waving lines. Cabinets and counter tops displayed unusual scientific paraphernalia. On a hook to the right was a head-set. He sat in front of a console in a swivel chair, and with a slight curl of, what could have been, amusement twitching at the corner of his mouth, he put on the head set and flipped on a switch.

"Can you hear me?" He spoke into the mouth-piece, adjusting a dial.

"I ... I ... Where am I? I can't see anything. I can't *feel* anything." A voice came through the head-phones.

"Good. Everything seems to be working correctly. You're in a laboratory. I need to ask you a few questions." After this brief introduction, the man in the lab coat pulled over some paper work and a pen. "Now, do you have any memories of your childhood?"

"Why can't I see anything? What's wrong with me? I can't even feel my breathing or my heartbeat."

The lab coat man sighed. He hated this part. He cleared his throat and tried for a clinical tone. "I'm afraid I have to tell you that, you're dead. Well, not all of you, obviously, but the person that you used to be is dead." He managed to sound matter-of-fact and without emotion: just flat information.

"Dead? How can I be dead when I'm still thinking. I'm still talking to you."

"Well, technically, X107, you're not talking to me. You are interfacing with me. You see, we have your brain hooked up to an Integrated Neural Stimulator. This new development allows us to communicate with a disembodied brain, which is what you are. You see, though the person you *were* is dead, your brain is still able to communicate. Now, if you'll let me continue, I have just a few questions for you."

"I'm not going to answer any of your questions until you answer a few of mine." The disembodied voice sounded agitated and demanding, angry even. "And my name is Albert Grimsby, not X-whatever. You say the person I was is dead? That doesn't make any sense. I'm obviously still thinking, still alive. You say I died? From what? How did I die? Damn it!"

"Renal failure. But, luckily, we were able to save a few of your parts."

"Ugh, I seem to remember that now. I was in the B Arnold Research Hospital. Yes, unfortunately, I do remember. ... I was dying." The disembodied voice seemed to fade off, dispirited and deflated.

Lab coat man continued in his efficient and clinical manner, "And now you are dead. But, just before passing, you graciously donated your body to science. Other organs of yours have been successfully transplanted into patients here at the hospital. You've saved lives. That should give you some comfort, and your brain is going to be used for very important research, X107."

"Stop calling me that. I'm Albert Grimsby!" The voice almost seemed to shout through the headphones. It resonated with anger.

"Not any more, I'm afraid," lab coat man said smugly. "You are just another donated organ from the body of Albert Grimsby. You can't be Albert Grimsby, you see, he's dead. But you have a number in our database, so we can differentiate you from the other brains. That's why I'm calling you X107."

"You mean there are one hundred and six other people in this horrible state besides myself?" The incorporeal voice rose in alarm.

"Oh, yes, there are many, many more brains that we are using for various experiments. You are among thousands."

"Thousands! This is terrible. This is inhuman! I didn't donate my brain to you people so you can experiment with it." The voice was extremely upset. "When I signed that donor sheet, I thought you might use my body for med school autopsy, or my heart and lungs and such for transplant. You have no right to use my brain in this way. How can you do this? It must be illegal."

Lab coat man heaved an exasperated sigh. Why do they always go through these delays? Such a bother. But he continued on according to his training, and that required him to calm the subject brain into a state of cooperation. He found it tedious, since the brain wasn't actually a person any longer.

"X107," he said, as patiently as he could muster. "You donated your body to science. That includes all the body parts. You can't un-donate it now. And since your body parts *are* donated to science, we are allowed to use these parts for experimentation."

"But I'm a thinking, feeling person ... or being, at least. What about my soul? What about my God given soul? Doesn't that go along with the part of the person that thinks, the part that has reason, the part that has memories?"

"I'm not concerned with the soul, X107. I'm a scientist. But your memories, now ..." lab coat man's tone changed to fervor. "That's exactly what I'm interested in. Now tell me, do you remember your childhood?"

"Yes, of course I remember my childhood. I grew up in Buffalo, New York. I had three sisters."

Lab coat man interrupted. "The details aren't necessary, X107. Just answer the questions, 'yes' or 'no'."

"How can the details be unnecessary? The details are my life. If you can preserve my memories, then at least I could see where this experiment would have some use. Why preserve my brain at all if you weren't interested in any of my memories?" The bodiless voice sounded truly perplexed.

"We are not interested in *you*, per se. You are only an organ for experimental purposes. The ultimate object of our experiments is to preserve the memories of those that have experienced important moments in history. Also, we are interested in preserving the mental capacities of the truly gifted, such as scientists, great philosophical or political thinkers, or great inventors and originators. I'm afraid, X107, you do not fall into these categories." Lab coat man droned on, as if what he said, somehow, made him even more important.

"I see," the disembodied voice said, as sad understanding came to him. "I'm not worth preserving. My memories are unimportant to anyone except me."

"On the contrary," lab coat said. "Your participation is invaluable. You will aid in the advancement of mankind. The questions I'm asking are to determine just how much of the usable brain has been retained. We need to know how well our preservation techniques are working, so far. So we can perfect our procedures for when we need to preserve a truly valuable brain. I'm sorry that we don't care about the actual content of your memories at this time, but your cooperation is important. In this experiment, X107, one of our aims is to realign our neural connections, to make future experiments optimally productive. You see, repetition of this experiment will increase the likelihood of ultimate success.

"And, I am pleased to tell you, that you are also to be a part of another, *very* important experiment." Lab coat man continued on, excitement rising in his voice. "We found, early on, that the brains in stasis could not be sustained for long periods. Then, finally, after the subject brains were interfaced with the Integrated Neural Stimulator, we discovered that the brains were able to be productively maintained for much longer periods. Communication with the brain was key. Without communication, the brain withers and dies.

"So now, we need to find out just how much interfacing is required, and how much down-time we can allow, to keep the brains active for the longest possible amount of time, without having them succumb to deterioration."

Lab coat man took a pompous breath and continued in a patronizing tone, "And that is where you come in, X107. You will be among ten selected brains that we will interface with at different scheduled periods of time. We need to see just how long the brains can remain active without communication. So, you see, you will be a very important part of achieving our ultimate goal."

"And you think I should care about this experiment? The bodiless voice asked. Well, I don't. To you, I'm nothing but a number, a piece of tissue without a soul. But you're wrong. And this treatment of your test subjects is wrong. This state you have me in is unbearable, you know. Without sight or hearing or feeling. Why, ... I'll go mad. I can't stand this, so called, stasis." The emotion in the bodiless voice sounded like extreme sadness, like it would cry if it could, if it had eyes. Then after a moment, the voice continued, "I guess, talking to you would be better than nothing."

"Now, that's the spirit," lab coat man said, sounding relieved. "Then I can count on your cooperation?"

"Wait a minute, before we continue. How often will you be communicating with me? How long will I have to wait?"

Lab coat man hesitated. He needed to get this part right. He checked his paper work. "Unfortunately, that's part of the test. I'm not allowed to tell you which of the time intervals you have been assigned for this experiment. But I am allowed to tell you that we definitely *will* resume communication with you at some point in the future, when your scheduled time has arrived. ... But, only if you cooperate now and answer all of my preliminary questions."

Albert Grimsby reluctantly had to agree. He didn't give two shits about their important experiment. And he actually felt that no one should have the right to use someone else' brain and invade their thoughts, after they had died. This experiment on brains was a travesty. And he would have refused to continue this charade on principle, but the time he had spent in stasis, before the voice of lab coat man had spoken to him was not something he could endure for long. It was, quite frankly, worse than death.

So Albert Grimsby answered all of the questions and reluctantly asked no more of his own. He cooperated as much as he was able. Then, after lab coat man disconnected the Integrated Neural Stimulator, Albert waited with patient desperation. He waited, floating insensate, without outside stimulation, in a hellish stasis. He waited for any word from his tormentors, any word.

After one week, three days, twenty-nine minutes, and six seconds had expired, lab coat man returned to the lab, sat in the swivel chair and switched on the Integrated Neural Stimulator.

STRANGE AND DISTURBING

With pen and paper at hand, he adjusted the dials, and checked in on the status of X107. After several vain attempts, he jotted down his findings:

> X107, brain subject
> Hopelessly insane
> Recommend termination and disposal.

Then, after completing this required task, he reached over to the console and dispassionately flipped off another one of the switches. There were only three left now, out of ten.

A GIFT FROM THE FAERIE PRINCE

THE GROUNDS OF MISERTON MANOR, JUNE, 1896

In the late afternoon, Mary Miserly was unexpectedly drawn into the woods that fringed the north portion of her estate. She had been taking a brisk walk across her expansive lawn in an effort to ease the tension brought on by the last two grueling hours she had spent going over her expense ledgers. And in her distracted mood, she had wandered a little farther along than her usual want, drawing perilously near to the woods and its unexplored shadows.

She had venture out this afternoon with no clear destination in mind, other than a need to remove herself from her secretary's office. It seemed every time she went over her books, she could envision her great wealth seeping through her grasp, and this made her stomach clench and her muscles knot. Exercise, she had hoped, would serve to calm her nerves and clear her mind.

Walking along the edge of the woods, her mind on her financial woes, she had noticed something glinting in the scant forest light, along the rim, of what appeared to be, a small path meandering through the trees. Whatever it was, it flashed a brightness, every now and then, and she was at a quandary to discern its nature from where she stood on the lawn. There was nothing to do, now that her curiosity was aroused, but to venture into the woods to discover what was causing this strange sparkle.

She hoisted up her long white skirts as she gingerly stepped along the path, not wanting to damage the fine material. But she wasn't too worried, since the path appeared to be wide and well-trodden, and she was sure to be careful.

She had gone ten small paces into the dense flora, when she spotted the shinning object that had aroused her attention, laying on the ground, perhaps another five more paces further on. Strange. She thought it had been closer to the edge of the forest than that, but the path was still clear all the way to the object, and so she moved a little farther into the woods.

Without taking her eyes from her chosen destination, she warily advanced to the spot where she knew she had seen the brightness just a moment before. But when she reached her goal and surveyed the area, she could find nothing hiding in the brush. Nothing to account for the shimmering reflection. She scythed her foot through the undergrowth, expecting to unearth a coin or perhaps a piece of lost jewelry, but she found nothing. Whatever it was, it seemed to have vanished and taken its twinkle along with it.

"Well, that was deuced strange," she said, to no one in particular. "I better not have dirtied my hem in this fruitless endeavor." And in a state of mild irritation, she turned to make her exit from the gloomy woods.

But when she looked around, she realized, she must have wandered farther into the forest than she had intended, for, from this spot, she could not see the welcoming lawns of her estate. She felt a little thrill of worry, and she hastily moved along the path retracing her steps. But after at least twenty paces more, she was still surrounded by forest, and appeared to be no closer to the open lawn. Her heartbeat quickened. She was becoming truly concerned. *It can't be far, now,* she thought. *I had only just stepped a short way into the woods.*

Trying to discern where she had gone awry, she glanced toward her feet to assess the direction of the path. Perhaps she had stepped unknowingly to the side. But, in a growing panic, she realized she could find no hint of a path in any direction.

Oh, my. Will I never get out of these damned woods? She began thrashing around through the brush, tearing her expensive skirts on the nettles, and catching her perfectly coiffed brown hair on the low lying branches. But after a half hour, she still was unable to find her way out, and her eyes filled with tears of frustration.

She was about to slump to the ground in dejection and exhaustion, and give herself over to a bout of weeping, when she saw a gleam of light breaking through the branches close by, hopefully indicating the possibility of a clearing.

"Oh, at last," she said, to no one in particular. And, in relief, she made her way toward the light.

STRANGE AND DISTURBING

But as she broke through the last tangled vegetation that obscured the clearing, she was hit by a feeling of profound disappointment. It was a clearing—true—but it was not her lawn. There, before her eyes, was a small hill, devoid of trees and brush, but covered in an expanse of fine waving grass. The hill was completely surrounded by forest, and at the top sat a beautiful dark haired man, of indeterminate age, dressed in the finery of a long ago time. He was alone and unarmed, and he wore a broad smile upon his handsome face. And yet, there was a menace about him that disturbed her and caused her already intense fear to heighten.

She was loath to show weakness in front of this stranger, for she knew it would put her at a disadvantage. She took a breath to summon her courage, and she spoke with bluster she did not truly feel. "Who are you? And what are you doing on my property?"

His bold smile worked its way into his eyes, frightening eyes. They seemed to burn with a strange green fire. "I do believe, lady, that this be not your property. You are now in my realm. This forest is mine."

"You are certainly an impudent one. I will ask you to leave," Mary said, in a haughty fashion, hoping to sound authoritative in this uncomfortable situation.

"You are not in a position to order me about, Mary. This is a faerie forest and it belongs to the faeries. I am Prince Oberon, prince of the faeries, and you are here at my behest." He inclined his dark head in a mock bow sweeping his arm in a graceful arc. Sparkles of iridescent light followed his fingertips through the air.

"You must be mad!" Mary looked around her in panic. Would she be safer scrambling through the woods?

As if he could hear her thoughts, he said, "Go ahead, my dear, Mary. Run. You will not be able to leave the faerie forest without my permission. But by all means ... do try. When you weary of the exercise simply call my name." Oberon leaned back into the grass on one elbow, careless of any damage to his fine apparel. He laughed, in a merry way, as her eyes opened wide in alarm. The laughter floated through the air like the tinkling of bright musical chimes.

Mary dashed back into the forest. She chose a direction she hoped was the right one. *Whoever he is, this man is obviously mad. And how does he know my name? Well, of course, he should know,* she thought. *He is on my property, after all.*

She thrashed through the forest, but she was having no luck leaving the accursed place. The more she fought against the brambles, the more tattered her dress became, the more disheveled her brown hair. And as she ran, she ruminated on Oberon's peculiar appearance. The man was certainly mad. Of that, there was no doubt. But what of those burning eyes? Did they not shine with an unusual and unnatural fire? What of that trail of brilliance he drew in the air? And the unmistakable sound of music when he laughed?

After another half hour of pointless wandering, Mary could see no other option than to try his suggestion. She doubted calling his name would help her any, not after she had spent such a long time stumbling through the deep growth, but she was now becoming desperate. She couldn't wander like this indefinitely.

"I suppose, I need your help, Oberon," she said in resignation.

Then, as before, she noticed a brightening in the woods, and she moved reluctantly in that direction. He sat on the hill, as before, patiently waiting for her return. "You see, Mary. You must stay in my realm until I release you."

"Very well. Then tell me: what is it you want from me?"

"I will take nothing from you. Rather, I wish to offer you a gift." There was a decidedly smug look on his face. Then his eyes narrowed. He didn't appear especially generous at that moment.

"You wish to give me a gift? Why?"

"Rest assured, I have my reasons," he said enigmatically. Then he continued, "You have discontinued the celebrations of the faerie festivals in the village. Your predecessor was always sympathetic to the ancient traditions. And yet, you chose to ban them. Why?"

"Not that it is any of your business what I do on my holdings, but those rites are pagan and dirty," she said, with distaste evident in her voice. "I do not believe they are wholesome for the common folk. And besides, they are wasteful and they cost money."

"You do not like to spend your money, do you, Mary?" he asked, with a smirk.

"You think my uncle was generous in his treatment of the villagers? Well, he wasn't so generous with me! Did he take me in when my parents died? Did he even provide for my welfare? My mother was his sister, and, just because she married a commoner, he cut her off. He left me to suffer for three years in a lowly orphanage. You would hold that man up to me as an example? It was his own nature that left him to die alone and unloved." From somewhere deep inside, Mary had found the energy to rise up in anger at the injustice of her early life. Her uncle had refused to give even a penny of his wealth to his sister; he had refused to give one ounce of his love to her.

"I had nothing in my youth. Nothing! When I struggled as a governess after leaving the orphanage, I was little better than a servant. I scrimped and saved. And, now that I, finally, have what is my due, I will not so easily relinquish what is mine, to spend on frivolities. The wealth I have now belongs to me, and I will do with it as I please."

The fire in Oberon's eyes turned cold. "A sad tale, to be sure, My Lady Mary, but one I have no sympathy for. Of your time at the orphanage, I have no interest. The concerns of humans are all too vain and mundane. But since you are the new Lady of Miserton Manor, I will tell you that, before you leave, you must choose." And again he swept his arm in a graceful maneuver, leaving a firey blaze of color in its wake.

There, before her on the grass, Mary saw two unusual items. To her left was a plain, yet curiously beautiful, key, made of some dull base metal. And to her right, an ornate chest, its lid open, filled with a large quantity of shimmering blue sapphires. These items had appeared from out of nowhere. "What is this?" she asked.

"Since your lands and our realm overlap, the faeries wish to offer you a gift. Please choose from the two items offered below. Take one with you and depart."

"And if I choose not to accept either one?"

Oberon shook his head at her obstinacy. "If you intend to ever leave the faerie forest, you must take one of these items with you."

Well, if she must, she must. It was better not to enrage a madman. And so, Mary bent down and scooped up the chest of brilliant sapphires. But, no sooner than she reached inside to touch the precious stones, then she found that the pile of shimmering blue had turned, by some enchantment, into mere water, and the liquid drenched her hand.

"But what is this?" she cried, and she turned her eyes back to the beautiful and dangerous looking man on the hill.

"You have chosen the chest of tears," Oberon said. "It is unfortunate, but it was, after all, your choice." And with a nod of his dark head, he informed her, "You are free to leave now. Go and take the chest with you."

"I don't believe that I want it," Mary said, and she bent to drop the offending gift onto the ground. But when she straightened back up, the heavy chest was still in her hands. The more she tried to let it go, the more attached it seemed to become. "Take this thing back," she demanded.

"The chest of tears is yours," Oberon said sadly. "Your home lies in that direction." And he pointed to a wide path that had opened in the greenery.

Mary stumbled away down the path, relieved to have a clear route through the undergrowth, and shortly she emerged back onto her own expansive lawn. "Thank God," she breathed. "I'll never go into those accursed woods again."

Mary started the long trek back to her manor house. She had to drag the heavy chest of tears, still attached to her hands, along with her. In distress, she looked down at the offending weight, and was surprised to find her hands appeared empty, yet she knew the evil item was still attached. The heavy chest was a burden that grew worse with every step she took.

Mary resumed her tedious life at the grand manor she had inherited from her dead uncle. Day after day, was spent worrying over her newly acquired wealth, afraid that it would inexplicably disappear and leave her once again destitute. She penny-pinched on the household expenses, and the house staff became resentful. She increased the tithes her tenants were obliged to pay, and they became disgruntled. She held no social gatherings, no elaborate balls, for fear of spending her wealth, and thus the social crowd, that she should have been a part of, became distant. And because she discontinued the faerie festivals, the villagers became unhappy and unwelcoming.

Over all, Mary's life was full of tension and loneliness. And, therefore, she was becoming a shrew and a spinster. And all the while, Mary was forced to carry along with her the heavy chest of tears. And the weight of the chest was becoming a drain on her health.

Finally, she was so miserable and lonely that she despaired of ever finding happiness, even though her wealth had actually increased. She determined that she must rid herself of this burdensome invisible chest of tears, even if she had to bargain or plead with the faeries. She would even be willing to pay them to take this accursed chest off her hands. And with her mind made up, she dragged the heavy chest across her expansive lawn all the way to the edge of the woods that fringed the north portion of her estate.

When she reached the forest, she boldly entered, calling out for Oberon as she went. In short order, she noticed a brightening in the forest's gloom, and with stubborn resolution she broke through the brambles to find the small faerie hill that she had seen from her last trek through the woods. And there, on the top of the mound, sitting as if enthroned by the grass, was the haughty and disturbing faerie, Prince Oberon.

The prince had that same infuriating smirk on his face that she remembered from the last time. "Well met, Mary," he said smoothly. "And what, pray tell, brings you into my forest?"

"I have come to strike a bargain with you," she said, drawing herself up to her full height and lifting her chin. "I need to be rid of this accursed chest. What must I do for you to take it off my hands?"

The faerie prince sighed and shook his head, but he offered a solution. "Perhaps," he said. "You might be rid of it. But you would need to perform several tasks to make that possible. I'm sure you will not like them, but I can tell you of them, if you are willing to hear."

"Anything! I am willing to do anything to relieve this blight," she said. And then, "Well, within reason, of course."

Oberon considered her for a moment and then nodded. "Very well," he said. "First: you have done the Shire great wrong by disallowing the common folk their right to celebrate the grand faerie festivals. There is a balance that needs to be maintained between the world of man and the realms of faerie. And you have disrupted the natural order. Perhaps, if you were to make this right, that would surely please the faeries."

Mary's face showed distaste, but she said, "All right. I can do that."

"And since you need to make amends for the past, I would suggest that you make the celebrations grand. I'm afraid you will need to impress the faeries now, so make them as grand as possible."

The thought of the amount of money this would cost her, gave Mary a chill, but she agreed. "Alright. I agree. I'll reinstate the celebrations. Will that remove the chest of tears?"

"It will help," Oberon replied. "But you must do more. There is a need in this area for a new orphanage. The old one is deplorable. I believe if you were to build a new one for the unfortunate orphaned children, the faeries would look favorably on this and might grant your boon. And so, for your second task, you must build this orphanage."

The thought of such expense made Mary's head swim. This cure was indeed going to hard. But she knew she could not drag this heavy chest around any longer, and her vast wealth was not helping to make her life happy. "Fine, I'll build an orphanage." She exhaled with the effort. But, now that the agreement was made, it was strange but she felt much better.

"And …" Oberon added. "It would be good, if the orphanage you build, is the finest in the kingdom. That will go a long way to making the faeries happy."

Surely he was playing with her now, Mary thought. But, in for a penny, in for a pound, as they say. She reluctantly gave her assent. "Yes, Yes. Anything else?" She asked sarcastically, expecting nothing further.

"One more thing …"

Mary glared daggers at the handsome prince. *Will he never make an end to his demands?*

"And third: It wouldn't hurt for you to volunteer your time at the orphanage after it is built. Oh, for say, at least eight hours a week. Not so much time out of your busy schedule, surely. I think the faeries would be satisfied with that."

She stared at him in disbelief. "If I must, I must. Do we have an agreement then?"

Mary was feeling very put out. The faeries were asking an awful lot of her. She wished she could say, no. She balked at the notion of spending that much of her wealth, but she was obliged to make this unsatisfactory deal with the faeries. She really had no other recourse.

"After you have completed your end of the bargain: reinstating the faerie festivals, and building the best orphanage in the kingdom, and spending at least eight hours a week in volunteer service at same for the next five years, I'm sure the faeries will give you their blessing."

That was the final straw. "Five years!" she screamed. "Alright! Alright! I agree." And saying this, she turned and fought her way clear of the forest, dragging her ever present burden, the heavy chest of tears, along with her.

Mary upheld her end of the bargain with the faerie prince. She reinstated the celebration of the faerie festivals and helped to make them very grand, indeed. She donated mead and mummers at the Spring Festival, wood from her forests and ale at the Summer Festival, and decorations for the village, as well as small gifts for the village children, at the Yule festival. And, as a result, the villagers were happy again and welcoming toward her.

She built the orphanage that she had promised. And not just any orphanage, but the grandest, most modern, orphanage in all the kingdom. It was a place where the orphans could grow strong, get educated, and be healthy. And, as a result, the children there were happy and grew to love their benefactor.

And she dutifully spent her time in volunteer work at the orphanage as promised. But, as so often happens, she could not manage to get all the things done that she wished to accomplish in a meager eight hours a week. And, soon enough, she found that she was spending sixteen hours a week at the orphanage, and then twenty four hours. And as her time became more in demand, so too, did the need for her monies in the upkeep and the growing expense of operation that such a vast enterprise entailed.

She found that once her tight purse strings became unloosed, it became easier for her to part with more of her wealth. And indeed, she began to enjoy the pleasure of being generous. By and by, her giving nature was observed by the physician who came to attend the children. And after a time of mutual acquaintance, a romance developed between herself and Doctor Pleasance.

Mary had been so busy with her volunteer work and her new romance, she had failed to notice that she was no longer weighed down by the oppressively heavy chest of tears. At some point, she realized, the faeries must have unburdened her, and she was grateful. Her health had returned to her, and, with the love of the good doctor, she was now content and happy.

But to make everything truly right, she knew she needed to return to the enchanted forest of the faeries and thank Oberon in person. For to do otherwise would not be gracious. And with a light step and a full smile, she walked to the edge of her expansive lawn and headed toward the woods that fringed the north portion of her estate.

Again, she boldly entered the woods and called out to Prince Oberon, the master of the enchanted faerie forest. "I've come to pay my respects to you, Oberon, and to give you my thanks."

She walked deeper into the dense brush, unafraid and light of heart. And soon enough, she spotted a glow in the distance, a little further into the deep forest. Breaking from cover, she was once again faced with the familiar grass hill and the beautiful, yet daunting, figure that perched at its crest.

"Well met, Mary," Prince Oberon said, greeting her in a friendly manner. This time, the man seemed genuinely happy to see her. The air he exuded was companionable and welcoming. "And what, pray tell, brings you into my forest?" he asked with a warm smile.

"I have come to give you my thanks," she repeated. "You, and the fairies, have relieved me of that terrible burden: the chest of tears. I will forever be in your debt for letting me return that gift to you."

"Alas, Mary," Oberon said with true amusement dancing in his bright green eyes. "We did not take back the chest of tears, for that was not the gift that we had given you."

Mary frowned in complete confusion. "But you did. You gave me the choice between the key and the chest. You told me I must choose."

"Oh, you humans. You are truly an amusing lot." And Oberon threw his head back in merriment. Musical laughter settled over the hill and rang through the trees. "The gift you were given was not the chest of tears. That gift you had given yourself, Mary. The faerie's gift, that you were given, was the opportunity to experience and choose between the two. You see, when the heavy weight of the chest of tears was gone from you, Mary, it was you who had finally put it down."

Oberon opened his arms toward Mary in a gesture of love and acceptance. "You have pleased the faeries by reinstating the festivals, by building the orphanage, and by donating your time to the children. But you have always had the blessing of the faeries, my lady. Go. Retrieve the key, Mary, for it is the gift that you have now given to yourself." And saying this he shimmered into a brilliant shaft of light, then slowly dissipated into the surrounding air.

Mary stared in thoughtful silence for several moments. Then a light appeared—not in the forest—but inside her soul. Satisfied with her conclusions of the encounter, and satisfied also with herself, she bent and picked up the key. Then exiting the woods that fringed the north portion of her estate, she walked with a determined stride, across her expansive lawn, and toward the best orphanage in the kingdom, firmly grasping the key to happiness in her hand.

THE MAN WHO COULD WALK THROUGH WALLS

It was another incredibly hot day in the desert of north central Mexico. El Chico Imeanest was finding the dry air uncomfortable. His skin was beginning to itch, and, just last night, he had a bloody nose. If he had to stay here any length of time, he might do something even worse than the crimes he had already committed. But it was plain that this was the prison where they had decided he should serve out his sentence: Prison Mas Fuerte, a huge maximum security fortress in the middle of nowhere, surrounded by miles of desert. It was a Godforsaken hole of a place, a scorched and barren hell on earth.

Why they would choose this place? Because of the super thick outside wall, the fancy gringo electronic technology? Or, perhaps, because it was located in the middle of an area controlled by his rival, Jose Ocampo and away from his own territory of Mexico City, which was the location of his home, his cartel, and most of his influence? Maybe. But he suspected that they believed their own hype, that there had never been a successful breakout from this prison, that this Godforsaken prison was impregnable and inescapable.

Up until now, El Chico was a legend among the prisons of Mexico. It was said, that he had the magical ability to walk through walls because he had escaped from every other prison where they had tried to contain him. And, eventually, he was sure, he would escape from this dried up rock as well.

He was also sure the authorities were wrong in assuming he had no influence in Chihuahua. Oh, no. They would find out, El Chico had friends everywhere. They could incarcerate him in Antarctica, and he would find the help he needed to escape. They would also find out that it was true: there was no prison ever made that could hold El Chico Imeanest.

He sat down at the visitor's table and faced his subordinate, but trustworthy, friend, Miguel, AKA El Gordo, so named because of his rather large girth and his profuse sweating. It was unbelievably hot in the visitor's hall, but El Chico remained dry. It was his pleasure to make other men sweat, especially men who were much larger than him. At four foot eleven, El Chico was as small as a child, yet he was one of the most feared men in all of Mexico. He watched the fat man squirm a little in his seat, and it was satisfying to watch Miguel in discomfort. He nodded at Miguel and waited for the good news he was expecting.

"Well?" El Chico prompted. There was no need to say anything else; Miguel would know what the boss wanted to hear.

"It's not going to be as easy as those other prisons. They have cameras everywhere here, motion detectors, and lots of other electronic contraptions. There's twice as many armed guards and they have men that walk around the perimeter every day with ground sweeping radar so they can find any tunnel we might dig. And besides that, there's flat land, with nothing on it but creosote bush and mesquite for miles around. We can't get near this prison without being seen." Miguel's voice crawled higher and higher in his agitation. To El Chico, he was starting to sound like a whining woman.

El Chico drummed his fingers on the table and calmly stared at Miguel. "It is imperative that I am out of this hell hole as soon as possible. I don't want to hear any excuses. I don't care what you have to do. Who you have to threaten. Who you have to bribe. But you will get me the hell out of here, and soon, or I will see to it that people die. ¿Comprendes?"

The incredibly hot temperature in the visitation hall, as well as his state of intense nervousness, was making Miguel sweat buckets. He dabbed at his forehead with his bandanna, a useless effort since the rag was already drenched.

"But ... we have an idea, El Chico," he stammered, hoping the boss would be pleased with what he was going to say. "It is a bit strange and could be very risky. But it will be a daring feat that has never been tried before, and one that the guards will never suspect. This escape will make you a legend. But it is not without danger."

Again, the only response from El Chico was a cold stare. There was no hint of any warmth in his eyes. It was said, to look into the eyes of El Chico, was to look into the eyes of a viper: into the eyes of death. Miguel felt death lurking over his shoulder, and his hands began to twitch.

"I am already a legend," the boss said.

STRANGE AND DISTURBING

Miguel took a deep breath for courage. He might as well say it and get it over with. "We know these guys, see, these scientists, who are working on this fancy machine. They call it a Molecular Displacer. You see they lost their funding from the US government, and our ... er ... *your* organization took over their research. We thought it would come in handy for other purposes. But anyway, they've developed this machine, see, this ... You remember that TV show about outer space? Viaje a las Estrellas? You know, Star Trek?"

El Chico slammed his fist down on the table. The guard at the end of the room glanced over, watching El Chico with intense scrutiny, waiting for trouble. But El Chico slowly removed his hands from the table, put them down at his side, and leaned back in his chair, indicating to the armed man at the end of the hall that he was not going to cause any further commotion.

"Madre de Dios," He hissed under his breath. "Get to the point El Gordo. You're trying my patience."

Miguel gulped down the spit that had lodged in his throat and continued, after another mop of his forehead. "This machine these guys developed, boss, it's like a transporter kind of thing. It will pluck you out of your cell and drop you somewhere else. ... Well, not drop you. ... Place you somewhere else, somewhere outside the prison, and we'll be waiting for you." He could see the interest in El Chico's eyes. Perhaps the boss was—maybe—a little pleased. Miguel let out the breath, he didn't even know he was holding, and ventured a slight smile. Then he added, "But it's not quite ready yet."

The interest that fleetingly graced El Chico's face morphed into disappointment. "Not ready yet? When will it be ready?"

"Well these Goddamn scientist guys have to do more experiments, they say. They have to work out a few bugs. They don't have the range they would like on this freakin' thing yet, but they're close. They say it will be all good, very soon." Miguel nodded his head encouragingly while he waited for his boss's response.

"How soon, is soon, El Gordo?"

Miguel crossed his fingers under the table. "Maybe six months, boss. That's what they said."

El Chico stiffened in his seat. There was no way he was going to wait six months. "You tell those stinkin' scientists, you tell those sons of bitches, that they will get me out of here in one month. They'll find a way—experiments or no experiments—to get their Goddamn machine ready in that amount of time, or their families will be the ones who suffer."

An evil smiled curled at the corners of his mouth. If it was anything El Chico liked, it was threatening someone. And knowing he could easily follow through with his threats made him feel very powerful.

"I'll relay that message, boss. I'm sure by next week, those scientists will be able to give you a more satisfactory time line."

"See to it, El Gordo."

Miguel could detect a slight sense of approval in his boss' face, but, nevertheless, he felt the threat as well. He realized El Chico was done talking to him. And with a profound feeling of relief, he rose from the table and headed for the security door.

༺༻

A week and two days later, El Gordo Miguel was once again sweating in the chair in the visitor's hall at Mas Fuerte Prison. Though he was much more confident today than he had been the last time he was here, he couldn't help but feel nervous. His breakfast squirmed around in his belly. Facing El Chico always made his bowels feel loose.

In his hand he held a thin chain, on which dangled some kind of strange medallion. He had managed to sneak it through security by telling the guard it was a gift from El Chico's hermana. The guard had looked it over, then had given it back to El Gordo Miguel with a nod. The image on the medallion was of an ancient Aztec glyph, and the guard had looked upon it with disapproval. Miguel didn't care what the guard thought as long as he was allowed to give this important item to El Chico.

With a grating metallic sound, a door on the opposite wall slid open, and El Chico was ushered into the hall, his leg chains dragging. He was accompanied by a large and unfriendly guard who motioned him into the chair opposite Miguel.

"How is everything, El Gordo?" the boss asked, as he sat down, smiling in a seemingly friendly manner. There was no sense of trouble, so the guard moved off toward the other end of the hall.

"Bueno, bueno. Our scientific friends have agreed—after a bit of persuasion—that the time for experimentation is done. They have agreed to attempt the final 'experiment' next week." Miguel's face was smug under a film of sweat. "I have a gift for you from your sister, Maria. She asks that you wear it while you are in this prison. It will give you luck."

As the gift was handed over to El Chico, the guard watched them closely, prepared to take action if needed. "Gracias, El Gordo, I will be sure to wear it." Without being told, El Chico knew that wearing this medallion was part of the plan for his escape. His sister, Maria, hated his guts and would never have sent a gift to him in prison. The only thing she was likely to send him was her wish that he rot here for the rest of his days.

Miguel nodded toward the piece of expensive looking jewelry. "She said to keep it close to your heart."

"I will, El Gordo. Now, tell me about my friends."

"Your 'friends' told us we have to set up something rather elaborate, since they have not been able to increase the range on the machine in such a short time."

A worrisome frown creased El Chico's brow.

Miguel continued, "Rest easy, boss. We have found a way to work around this." Miguel leaned forward just a little. "The prison has contracted to have metal pillars, containing ground penetrating sonar, sunk into the grounds around the outside wall. They hope to be able to detect the minute sounds of tunneling with these devices. "It is a tribute to you, boss. They know your reputation; that you have escaped every other prison; that it is said you can walk through walls. They have spent very big bucks to be the prison from which there is no escape. But we will turn this plan against them."

El Chico seemed very pleased. "You have people in this construction crew? Our own men?"

"No, boss. They had already contracted some company from the city of Delicias to do the work. And there's no way we can leverage someone from this company in such a short time. But we will not need their help. You see, we will sabotage their drill rig. Then, in order to get this project completed by the deadline, they will be forced to rent another piece of equipment. And ... that new drill rig—which will conveniently be the only one nearby—will conceal the scientist's machine, the molecular displacer, the transporter."

"I like it." El Chico smirked. "Then these other people will be held culpable."

"Hopefully, no one will ever know how it was done. You will simply have vanished."

El Chico was very pleased, indeed. After this unbelievable escape, his legend would grow. Everyone would fear El Chico Imeanest. And then he would be unstoppable.

As El Chico looked off toward the corner with a disturbing smile on his face, Miguel continued, "We only need to get the machine close to the prison walls for it to be in range. This work—the drilling of the holes for the sonar tubes—is scheduled to take three days. But once the drill rig is in place, on that very first night, the scientists will be able to remotely trigger the transporter machine. As per the plan, we will have our men waiting, hiding in the desert at some distance outside the prison walls. They will intercept you after you have been transported, and take you to the small helicopter we have concealed about five miles from Mas Fuerte.

"As far as anyone will ever know, you will simply have disappeared from your cell in the middle of the night. And by the time the guards are aware of your absence, you will be well on your way to Mexico City."

El Chico had to chuckle. "Everyone will believe I magically walked through the walls."

But then his face became very serious. The cold, snakelike look in his eye frightened Miguel, as the boss lowered his voice to a menacing hiss. "I don't want anyone to ever find out how I escaped from this prison. As soon as the scientists have completed their 'experiment', I want them dealt with. ¿Comprendes?"

Miguel's guts felt liquidy. He knew El Chico didn't get to be the boss by being soft, but this order was heartless and, to Miguel's mind, unwise. These scientist guys could have been useful in the future. But he knew not to question the boss.

"Whatever you say," Miguel agreed. He tried not to show his disappointment. "One other thing: the scientists need you to wear that medallion in order to locate you, so keep it on."

El Chico narrowed his eyes at Miguel. "I got that, El Gordo."

After Miguel left, El Chico was escorted back to the security door. He took the cross he had always worn from around his neck, and, in its place, he hung the Aztec medallion. As he left the visitor's hall he dropped the old crucifix in a trash bin.

⁂

In the desert surrounding the prison of Mas Fuerte, the air had taken on a sharp chill. Six of El Chico Imeanest's most trusted asociados huddled behind the scrub bushes that dotted the bleak terrain. Each man wearing desert camo and night vision glasses. They waited in silence for the moment when the Molecular Displacer would be remotely engaged, and their boss, El Chico Imeanest, would be transported from his prison cell. It was their job to locate him as quickly as possible, cover his prison garb with a camouflage jumpsuit, and spirit him off to the waiting helicopter.

At three o'clock in the morning, the machine was remotely activated, and shortly after, the scientists who had worked so diligently for El Chico's release were promptly dispatched. At this same time, the asociados outside the prison began their search for El Chico. They combed the area outside the prison. But after two hours of search and no evidence of the boss being found, it was assumed that there must have been a malfunction in the Molecular Displacer machine. At five ten in the morning, they heard the piercing sound of the prison sirens scream across the desolate Chihuahuan Desert, and the men retreated, as quickly as they could, away from Mas Fuete Prison.

Upon finding El Chico missing from his cell, the prison of Mas Fuerte immediately went into lock-down. Guards searched the prison complex, inside and out. Sodium lights scraped over the desert scrub. Then, at five thirty, one of the guards thought he saw a man at the base of the outside wall. The large searchlights of the prison were directed to the spot where the man had been spotted. And to the warden's immense relief, that man was identified as El Chico Imeanest.

... Well, not all of El Chico. Only half of the famed outlaw could be seen, for that was the half that protruded from the prison's great outside wall. His other half, it could only be assumed, was still inside the wall. Everyone was in shock and could find no explanation. How could this have come about? Was the man really able to walk through walls?

The guards came to believe that he could. A rumor was told among them, of how El Chico was seen dropping his crucifix into the trash and donning a pagan symbol. They told the story of how God had become displeased with El Chico, not because he was a crook, not because he was a murderer, but because he had turned his back on the God of his youth. And that God, in his anger, took away El Chico's gift of being able to walk through walls. And, in His righteousness, he took this gift away at the very moment before the outlaw's escape.

The prison authorities never did remove El Chico's remains. They felt it was fitting that he remain entombed, with half of his body rotting on the outside of the prison wall, where one eye could tantalizingly see freedom, but, nevertheless, where he would always remain a prisoner. It is said that they left this grizzly reminder as a warning to everyone that this was the consequence of a life of crime. But it was also said, that the decomposing limbs were the prison's trophy. And by this gruesome display, it boasted to the world, and to the criminals of Mexico: it didn't matter who you were ... there would be no escape from Mas Fuerte Prison.

THE CHICKEN FOOT TALISMAN

After walking up and down Bourbon Street for the last hour, Alfie was getting tired and thirsty. "How about if we stop in at one of these cute bistros and have one more cold one, then call it quits for the day?"

George gave Alfie a sidelong look. "You can't be tired yet. We have the whole afternoon to see the sights. Besides, we just had lunch an hour and a half ago, and we each had three drinks. I'm still feeling the buzz."

Alfie looked miserable. His sparse hair was damp, and his glasses were steaming up. "It's hot and humid, George. My shirt's starting to stick to my back."

It really was getting hot, but George wanted to get his full experience of New Orleans before they left town. They were only going to be here for a couple of days at the hardware convention at the Ritz. He wanted to have some fun this afternoon, before they had to go back to the hotel and listen to some more boring demonstrations.

Boy, he thought, *I sure picked the wrong buddy to perambulate with. Jeez.* George was thinking this guy was a real stick-in-the-mud. "Okay," he conceded. "Let's head over to Dauphine and we'll stop at a bar over there on our way back to Canal Street. I think Dauphine is one block that way. Can you make it that far, Alfie?" George asked, sarcastically, and he pointed to the left, down another quaint French Quarter street.

The buildings on Conti Street looked very interesting, to be sure. It seemed to have all the character of Bourbon Street, but without the crowd. Maybe it wouldn't seem as God awful hot, Alfie thought, without so many people breathing down his neck. Well, he supposed, another block or two wouldn't kill him. But before he continued, he wanted a promise from George, so he stopped in his tracks on the corner.

George was so full of energy, still a young man, it made Alfie tired just to look at him. The guy wanted to stop at every bar and check out all the girls; he thought he was some kind of Don Juan the girls couldn't resist. Alfie was afraid George's unbridled enthusiasm might cause him to veer off on a tangent along the way, and Alfie wanted to conclude this sightseeing tour. Soon. Right after he had a cold beverage.

"We stop at a watering hole on Dauphine, have one, and then head straight back. Just one more place, then back to the hotel, right?" he asked, before he would agree to move any further.

"Promise," George said, rolling his eyes.

Alfie reluctantly moved along. As soon as they were out of the crush, he immediately felt cooler. He liked this street better than Bourbon. It wasn't as maddening or as noisy, but it had that New Orleans charm. Some of the buildings were stucco, and painted in colorful pastel shades which brightened his mood. A brick building, farther down the block, had balconies overlooking the road and embellished with ornate wrought iron railings. To Alfie, it looked just like a post card.

About halfway down the street, with Dauphine in sight, Alfie spotted a small gift shop with some voodoo dolls on display in the window. He had just remembered that he had promised to buy his mother a souvenir from his trip to the Big Easy, and he hadn't gotten around to shopping for it yet. Besides, he really felt he needed to get out of the sun for a while, or he was sure he was going to hurl.

"Let's stop in here for a minute, George. I need to get something for my mom."

"I thought you were in such a big hurry to have a drink?" George laughed. "Sure. This place looks cool. I didn't know your mother was into this kind of thing, but, whatever. Maybe I'll buy something too."

As they entered the unusual little shop, a small bell attached to the door frame tinkled, announcing the presence of customers to a woman sitting behind a counter just inside the door.

"Good afternoon, gentlemen." Her rich voice rose melodiously into their ears. It sounded as exotic as a Caribbean bird. And, like a rare bird, she was as brilliantly garbed. She wore a silk caftan with a wild colorful print, and she had a turban of silk, in an entirely different pattern, wrapped around her head. She jingled, as layers of gold hued necklaces swayed about her neck, and six very large hoop earrings clanked against each other. "What can I help you wid today?" she asked.

George glanced over at Alfie and raised his brows. As exciting as she might appear, her voice sounded bored and vaguely annoyed. "Just looking," he said.

And hearing this, the woman waved them into the strange shop with a heavily ringed hand. Then she turned her attention back to whatever she was doing before the men intruded.

The two men wandered around the store looking at the bizarre items offered for sale. They didn't really believe that this was a genuine voodoo shop, not here in this district. But these freaky voodoo things were probably just the kind of souvenirs the tourists wanted, and this area was certainly full of tourists.

The store was full of jars with labels that claimed they contained strange herbals or other gross sounding stuff. One jar contained, according to the label, ground black cat bone. Another had alligator skin. And hanging from a dowel suspended between two laminated tree branches, was a selection of talismans dangling from chains. The place was definitely full of oddities, and the men walked around the shop gawking and laughing at the peculiar wares. Occasionally, the woman's dark eyes would look up from behind the counter and stare at the two men with a disapproving squint.

George began to feel uncomfortable. "This store has some really creepy stuff in it. I don't think this is my cup of tea," he called out, and he glanced over at Alfie, who was staring at the row of talismans suspended from the dowel. "Let's continue on to Dauphine. I think I'm getting thirsty now too."

Alfie held one of the strange pendants in his hand, and he looked over at the brightly plumaged woman behind the counter. "What's with this claw thing?" he asked.

She gave him a casual patronizing smile. "Ah, yes. Dat be de lucky chicken foot. I sell a lot of dos."

"Is it guaranteed to bring you good luck?" he asked. Alfie seemed interested enough to actually make a purchase.

"Some say," she nodded. "But maybe good luck ... maybe bad," she added noncommittally

Well, of course, she wouldn't promise good luck, Alfie thought. She couldn't really guaranty anything. Could she? But, fake or not, Alfie found this item intriguing, and he decided he was going to buy it for himself. He planned to tell his friends back home that he got it from a real voodoo priestess. They'd never know the difference. Of course, he'd have to find something else for his mother. Something more 'mother friendly'. Less strange.

"I'll take it," he said.

"You must be nuts," George said, shaking his head at Alfie. "It's probably not even a real chicken foot. It's probably vinyl or plastic. And, besides, it looks creepy, my friend."

Alfie didn't listen to George. He had a good feeling about the chicken foot, and he didn't care what George thought; he thought it was cool. So he paid for the talisman, and he and George left the shop in search of a bar on Dauphine.

Just as they reached the corner, a large sound system speaker got nudged by a reveler's foot. It fell off of a second story balcony railing, where someone had foolishly placed it, and it began its deadly descent to the ground below. It came whooshing through the air, dropping to within an inch of Alfie's head, where it dangled momentarily on its own wire, before continuing its inevitable plunge. In that split second before the wire broke, Alfie managed to duck his head to the side.

The speaker smashed into smithereens, and George stared in horror at his friend, who was holding his chest and gulping in air. "My God," he said. "You could have been killed! It hovered over your head just long enough for you to move out of the way. Cripes, that was close. I definitely need a drink now."

"Me too," Alfie said, feeling more shaken than he wanted to admit.

So the two men went into the first bar they came upon on Dauphine Street. The front of the establishment was completely open to the street by three large overhead doors, and fans were whirling at the top of a high ceiling. The place looked cool and inviting, but it was teaming with tourists. There was a long bar along the left side wall, and it looked pretty full up. But, as luck would have it, they spotted two empty stools at the near end, and they made their way through the maze of tables to the two spots that seemed to be waiting just for them. They sat at the bar, and each ordered a double shot of bourbon.

Alfie no longer felt tired. With the adrenaline pumping, he was as wired as George, and he was feeling very alive. He was really going to enjoy this drink.

Before they could finish their bourbon, a group of eight, incredibly pretty, young women entered the bar. The guy that was sitting next to Alfie, finished his drink and got up, leaving the bar stool empty. Then, the prettiest of the eight, a tall slender blond, sat down on the stool next to Alfie and gave him an encouraging smile.

George nudged his friend with his elbow, and gave him an envious smirk. "That talisman you bought is certainly working for you, man. I think it's giving you good luck. Maybe I should go back and buy one."

"See. And you thought I was crazy for buying it," Alfie said, with a smug grin.

"Tell you what, Alfie. You sit here with this bevy of beauties, and I'll be right back. I'm gonna get me one of those lucky chicken foot talismans." And saying that, George took his leave.

STRANGE AND DISTURBING

In the meantime, while he waited for George, Alfie was making friends with all the pretty girls, and he was having the time of his life. He was feeling so much better about New Orleans. The air no longer seemed too hot for him. No, it was just right. And he was feeling lucky, blessed and lucky. The chicken foot was giving him an unaccustomed aura of self-confidence. He could sense the girls responding to his new charisma. They were enjoying his conversation and laughing at all his clever remarks. This was, indeed, his lucky day. He forgot all about George.

After about a half hour of flirting and drinking, he heard a commotion out in the street. One of the girls looked out and said, "Looks like someone's been hit by a car."

Everyone in the bar went to the doors and windows to gape at the spectacle. When Alfie looked out, he was shocked to see that it was his friend, George, lying in the street. There was a crowd milling all around him, and someone was giving him first aid. Thank God, he wasn't dead. But he appeared to be badly hurt, and he was bleeding profusely. Alfie rushed out to be near his friend, and help in any way he could. He told the first aid guys that he was the injured man's friend, and they let him kneel by George, while they waited for the ambulance. Alfie noticed that a chicken foot talisman was in his friend's hand.

The crowd of onlookers grew larger, and Alfie could feel them staring, and hear them talking among themselves. He heard someone in the crowd say, "It was the chicken foot talisman. Sometimes they bring good luck, they say. But, sometimes, they can bring bad luck."

Alfie became concerned. Before the ambulance arrived, he took the chicken foot out of George's hand and he threw it to the side of the road. Then, without anyone noticing, he placed his own talisman in his friends hand and, leaning toward his ear, he said, "You need the good luck now, my friend, more than me."

As the ambulance took off down Dauphine, carrying two unfortunate New Orleans tourists, a young woman, wearing an outfit as colorful as a peacock and an unusual amount of jewelry, walked to the side of the road. She pulled a glove from a hidden pocket, and mumbled, "I hate tourists," under her breath. She donned the glove and scooped up, what appeared to be, a shriveled claw attached to a metal chain.

"I sell dis bad luck chicken foot to some other sucker," she said, as a wicked smile spread over her face. Then, wrapping the claw up in her handkerchief, she headed down Dauphine and turned right onto Conti Street.

"Dey be such assholes, deez tourists," she said, shaking her head. "I swear, dey will believe anyting!"

THE MADHOUSE

Harold woke up to strange surroundings. It took all of his effort to open his eyes, and when he did, he recognized nothing. He sat quietly in his chair, glancing around the room, trying to get his head around what he was seeing.

He was in a large room that he knew he'd never seen before. The walls were gray, the floor was beige, and the ceiling was white: altogether a very uninspiring space. It could be anywhere ... except for the bars on the windows.

There were other occupants in the room, he noticed, and his eyes scanned over them with interest. Most were sitting in chairs, like himself, some slumped over in uncomfortable positions, some apparently playing cards, one staring at the wall. Another two occupants were pacing the floor, mumbling to themselves. All of them were wearing hospital robes.

As his mind cleared out the last of his sleep, he realized, with some concern, that he must be in a hospital. And by the look of the other patients, he figured it must be some kind of a mental hospital. He sat up straight in his chair. Suddenly, a feeling of panic washed over him. What could have happened? Why was he in a madhouse? Oh, no, no, no! This can't be right. He wasn't crazy.

He looked around for a nurse or an orderly and finally spotted someone who looked likely to be a nurse, over by the door. He got up slowly, realizing he was still a little dizzy—sleep had apparently not been completely shaken off—and he headed determinedly in the direction of the door.

"Excuse me. Excuse me, nurse, but there is definitely some mistake here."

The nurse turned to him with a tolerant smile, wherein lurked the hint of recognition, and asked, "Yes, Harold? What seems to be the problem?"

A clawing suspicion grabbed at Harold. This woman knew his name, and yet, he did not recognize her in the least. Just what was going on here?

"There's been some kind of mistake. I don't belong here. I'm not sick. I need to speak to someone in authority."

"Calm down, Harold, everything's all right. You're in St. Gerald's Mental Hospital, dear. Now, you know that." The nurse reached out and gently took him by the arm. "Why don't you come back over here and have a seat, and calm down. You're safe here, and everything is as it should be."

What the hell is wrong with her? He thought. Obviously, everything was *not* as it should be. He wasn't supposed to be here. He didn't belong here.

Then he realized that, whatever *was* going on, she must be in on it. It wouldn't do him any good to argue with this woman, he thought. He looked straight at her, the better to judge her facial expressions, and said, "I need to speak with someone in authority. And I need to see them, now."

He sat down in the chair where the nurse had indicated, pretending to be cooperative. It wouldn't do to make a ruckus at this time, he figured. So, he'd pretend to play along until he could find some answers. But first, he would assess the situation.

"Of course, you can speak to the Doctor, Harold. When he comes in. He'll be making the rounds in this ward in about another hour." She patted his hand in a patronizing way and turned to leave him there in the chair.

An hour? Harold felt that panic starting to bubble up in his throat again, and he had to deliberately try to squelch it.

"I'm afraid that I can't wait an hour, Miss. I demand to see him immediately." He said this with as much dignity and calm as he could muster. His natural instinct was to rush at the door and attempt to flee, but his reason prevailed. That kind of action would probably get him nowhere.

The nurse's friendly attitude became strained. She drew in a long loud inhalation, forcibly speaking in a composed voice; impatience and annoyance lurked behind her eyes. "You sit quiet now, Harold, and wait for the doctor, or I'll have to call in the orderly. You don't want me to do that, now do you, Harold?" Her expression changed back to compassion, and she gave his hand a gentle pat. Then she turned and walked away, shaking her head.

Harold's thoughts were churning. What was going on here? At first he assumed it was some kind of a mistake, but now he dreaded that this was all deliberate, a scheme to lock him away. What could be the purpose? He wasn't rich. They couldn't be after his millions; he didn't have any. Had he seen something he shouldn't?

STRANGE AND DISTURBING

Were crime bosses set on shutting him up? Or, maybe, he had inadvertently gotten involved in some international intrigue. He was clueless as to why anyone would want to put him away, but there was definitely a plot of some kind going on here.

A nasty thought occurred to him. What if the doctor was in on it as well? He'd have to be careful when he spoke to him, feel him out. Harold thought he'd be able to tell if the doctor was suspect by watching his face. He decided that, he'd calmly talk to the doctor and see what he had to say. If he seemed in cahoots, he'd remain calm and form a different plan for his escape. At least he wasn't in isolation. If he had to, maybe he could slip a note to one of the visitors of the other patients. *Think, Harold. Think. Remain cool and unflustered and bide your time,* he told himself. *You'll get out of this.*

The hour passed with Harold still trying to figure out what had happened, and what he was going to do about it. The doctor finally came in, and the nurse approach him immediately. She glanced, surreptitiously, in Harold's direction, and the doctor nodded as he listened. She was, obviously, attempting to sway the doctor's opinion. But what was she telling him? Harold's heartbeat quickened, and he gulped air in angry bursts. He struggled to get his emotions under control. *Calm down,* he told himself. *You must remain calm.*

Sure enough, the doctor headed in his direction first, then he stopped in front of Harold's chair, looking down at him expectantly, his hands in his big white pockets. There was a stethoscope around his neck.

"I understand you wanted to see me, Harold? What seems to be the issue?"

Harold got a definite sinking feeling. "You know me?" he asked. "You used my name. You know who I am?"

"Yes, of course, Harold. You've been a patient here for three years. Have you forgotten who you are, again?"

Harold could feel anger trying to take hold of him. That was a bold faced lie that the doctor was telling. Harold was sure he'd never seen this doctor before in his life. He wanted to holler back at the doctor and accuse him of the lie, but the guy was obviously in on the subterfuge, so he knew he would have to be very careful.

Maybe he wasn't even a real doctor. Maybe this whole scene was some kind of a charade. He knew he wasn't crazy. They were trying to trick him into questioning what he knew was real. If he didn't get out of here, they might really drive him crazy with this routine.

He looked around at the other patients in the room with suspicion. Were they a part of the scheme? No, he decided. After close scrutiny, they looked pretty genuine to him. One of them had a length of drool dangling out of the corner of his mouth. It had wetly strung itself out to become a glistening line from his mouth to the top of his hospital gown. No, the patients were real patients. But the doctor and the nurse? They couldn't be for real.

"I know who I am," Harold said, with strained composure. "The question is: what am I doing here?"

The doctor pulled a chair over to sit in front of Harold. "At the moment, you're not well, Harold. You need to be taken care of. We, here at St. Gerald's, are doing just that. We want what's best for you." He spoke in a genuine manner.

STRANGE AND DISTURBING

This guy is really good, thought Harold. *He almost appears to be telling the truth. Except that, I know he's full of shit.* Harold had to tamp down the urge to scream back at the doctor. He could feel his fragile control slipping away. He wanted to grab the guy by his white collar and threaten him with bodily harm, but he stayed in his chair, seething in his quietude.

The doctor pretended to listen to his heart and check his eyes, then asked him about his general health. Harold answered him through clenched teeth, in short hissing breaths. He was sure this whole doctor thing was a sham, but he played along because he felt he had to.

"Why don't you tell me a little bit about why you feel so angry today, Harold." The doctor said, after he completed his fake doctor show. "What's troubling you?"

What's troubling me? You've got to be kidding me, Harold thought. Suddenly, he just couldn't take it anymore. His anger at this injustice erupted into his face with the intensity of a house on fire.

"There is nothing wrong with me! Someone has put me here against my will and without my knowledge. I've never seen you, or any of these people, before. You're all lying to me. I demand an explanation. I demand to be let out of here, immediately!"

Harold had started this tirade a bit loudly and then crescendoed into shouting. He flung his arms wide in exclamation, then he poked an accusing finger hard into the chest of the doctor.

Too late, he realized the immense mistake he had just made. Two orderlies materialized out of nowhere and rushed to the doctor's aid. Harold panicked. He made a lunge for the doctor before the orderlies could reach him.

"Let me out of here," he yelled. Let me out. I'm not crazy!"

The orderlies each grabbed one of Harold's arms with titanium-like strength. They held him tight as he struggled.

"Calm down, Harold." the doctor said in a calm, quite voice, seemingly unaffected by Harold's outburst.

But Harold was too upset now to desist. Against his own better judgment, Harold kept up his angry outburst, accusing everyone of malfeasance, accusing everyone of subterfuge. And then, since he refused to calm down, the two orderlies forcibly removed him from the room, kicking and screaming. He was dragged down the hall, taken to a small room, and strapped down in a chair.

This was too much, thought Harold. When he got out of here, he would see to it that every one of these brigands paid for this indignity. And they would pay dearly. ... If he ever got out of here. He yelled, and screamed, and thrashed around, until he was exhausted. Finally, he quieted, more from lack of energy than anything else. And, after several hours, he again was able to converse with the attendants in a civil manner. He promised them his good behavior, and they unfastened him from the chair. After several more hours, with no further outbursts, they told him they would return him to the recreation room where he could join the other patients. But he was to remain on his best behavior, or else ... they would be forced to remove him once again.

He would have to keep his temper under control, until he could find a way out of here. He sat back down in the chair he had originally woke up in. The other people around him really were crazy. He could see that plain. But he, himself, was not. Tomorrow, he thought, he'd see if any visitors arrived for one of these nutcases, then he'd see if he couldn't slip one of them a note.

Yes, he would try that route tomorrow, he mused, since it was sure that he'd get no help from the staff.

Satisfied that he had a good working scheme in his head for solving this problem of his erroneous incarceration, he leaned his head back in his chair, attempting to tranquilize his intractable agitation. He closed his eyes, blocking out the view of the offending 'hospital' and drifted off to placid sleep.

⫷⫸

After what seemed like days, Harold woke again. Looking around the room, observing all the strange figures lounging in chairs about him, he tried to shake the dizziness from his brain. A feeling of panic clutched suddenly at his heart when he noticed the bars on the windows. He didn't recognize this room. He didn't recognize these people. There was something very wrong, here. He took a closer look at the other occupants. Then he realized he was surrounded by crazy people.

"There must be some mistake," he said, in total incomprehension. "Where the hell am I?"

The nurse, by the door, looked over at Harold. She raised her brows and grimaced. Then she shook her head, as if to say, 'here we go, again.' And with a soft sigh of resignation, she slowly and purposefully walked in Harold's direction.

DNA SECRETS

"I remember the day the envelope arrived," Martin said, and then his face went blank. He appeared lost in thought, and then he shook himself and turned to his companion at the bar. "It had looked innocuous enough," he said. "I recall waiting with growing excitement for its arrival for four weeks, but after it had finally arrived, I wasn't so sure that I really wanted to know. Finding out about my background would be an important event in my life, you see. I never knew who my father was. So, originally, I had felt that, reading the results of my DNA test, would help me to fill in some blanks."

Fred listened politely. He had heard about these online DNA tests, and he was curious. He waited for Martin to continue.

"I had been raised by his mother, alone, a single parent. I had no complaints about how I was raised, you understand. I couldn't have asked for a better, more loving, parent than my mother. And I really didn't need a father. Having only the one parent had always sufficed, because my uncle lived in the same house with us. He had been there through all my formative years, so I didn't lack for a male role model. I didn't really care if my mother wanted to keep my father's identity a secret. Did it matter what his name was? I didn't think so. He never had any place in my life growing up. But as I grew older I came to wonder about my background, you know, my heritage."

Fred gave Martin an understanding nod. He could appreciate that someone would want to know about an absent parent. He sympathized with Martin's situation.

Martin cleared his throat. "Like I said, Fred, I didn't look anything like my mother, and I was curious as to what information I might find out about my unknown father."

It was obvious to Fred that something about this tale was disturbing for Martin. He watched the other man take a long drink of vodka before continuing.

"My mother was of Italian descent, and her hair was dark and luxurious. Yet what little hair I have is pale and thin. Look at my eyes. They're pale too." Martin turned to face Fred, showing him the truth of his statement. Martin's eyes were not only pale, they were strange looking in some undefined way. Unusual.

Martin continued, "And she was a large woman, both tall and husky. Yet here I am short and thin, almost frail. I was curious as to just where my father's people would have come from. So I sent away to this website, 'Your DNA Secrets' to have my DNA checked."

Fred inclined his head in consideration. "I was thinking of having my DNA done too," he said.

"Well, before you do ..." Martin gave Fred a warning look. "Just let me tell you what I found out.

"My mother never spoke of my father—not at all—and she would change the subject if I ventured to ask her anything about him. I always found it disturbing. And my uncle would just shake his head, claiming it wasn't his place to tell. Well, so fine, I thought. I don't care who he was, I just wanted to know *what* he was, like German or Scandinavian, or something. But even vague questions like that often made her angry. Then when I opened that envelope from 'Your DNA Secrets', I was taken completely by surprise. You know what it said?" Martin glowered at Fred like *he* had sent the offending letter.

"What did it say?" Fred prompted.

"Nothing! There was nothing there but a bunch of question marks."

"What?" Fred wasn't expecting this. He was a little confused. "So what does that mean?"

"Right? That was what I wondered. They had all the information I expected about my mother's DNA but not a damn thing about my father. I thought, this is bullshit. I paid two hundred dollars for that information. I marched over to my computer and brought up the 'Your DNA Secrets' website. I was going to give them a piece of my mind or get my money back, but that's when I made my big mistake. Well, you could imagine. I was pissed."

"What mistake are you talking about?" Fred asked. Martin lowered his voice in a conspiratorial tone and leaned over toward Fred. "You know they monitor the internet, don't you? Yeah, as soon as I made my complaint, I figured those guys honed in on it. ... Well, it might also have been when I bitched about it on social media. But anyway, they found out."

Fred looked at Martin in a cautionary way. He didn't know what to make of this turn in the conversation. "Who found out? What did they find out?"

"What I need to warn everyone about. Three days later, while I was surfing the internet, I heard my front door bell ring. I wasn't expecting anyone, so I went to the small window in the door and looked out." Martin's eyes shifted around the room as though he expected someone to be eavesdropping. "On my front porch stood two guys in suits. I'd never seen them before. They looked like some kind of missionaries, or something. I thought about ignoring them, and making like there was nobody home, but one of them spotted me in the window. So I opened the door, ready to give them the 'I'm not interested speech', but before I could get a word out, one of them says, 'Are you Martin Damarte?' 'Yeah,' says I, and they proceeded to budge their way into my house.

"The taller and uglier of the two guys reached into his jacket pocket and pulled out a business card. 'We're from SOBER,' he says. 'The Security Officials for the Bureau of Economic Revenue'. Well, I never heard of any such organization. But what the hell do I know? The guy said they were acting on my complaint about the 'Your DNA Secrets' website. Said, they just wanted to ask me a few questions. They wanted to look at the results from my DNA test. Then they asked me some damn personal questions. I got annoyed. Like, who did these guys think they were, anyway? I asked them to leave, and one of them stuck me in the neck with something. The next thing I know, I'm in the back of some nasty van, tied up and gagged and heading off to who knows where."

Fred was thinking of a good excuse he could use to get away from this conversation, when Martin's hand suddenly rested on his arm, and so he stayed seated on his bar stool. A cursory glance around the barroom showed no other friends of his in the area. Unfortunately, he felt obliged to continue listening.

Martin's voice turned desperate. "On the way to 'wherever', one of the guys comes clean and tells me that they are really members of the Secret Organization for the Total Termination of Extraterrestrial Descendants, and they were doing round-up missions for this SOTTED organization." Martin's strange eyes grew large and stared full into Fred's face. "Yeah, that's right," he nodded. "It turns out, I'm half alien. Like, my father was from outer space. And these guys were hell bent on terminating me."

"You don't say." Fred tried not to look at Martin askance, but it was clear that Martin must be one of those kooks you read about, and so he decided he'd had just about enough of his bullshit. It was time to make an exit, and this time he wouldn't let Martin stop him from leaving.

"Before you go," Martin said, with what appeared to be, a frightened look over his shoulder. "Take my card. I'm giving one to as many people as I can. The more people that know the truth about this SOTTED organization, and about what happened to me, the safer I'll be. They won't dare nab me now after I've told people the truth. Too many people will get suspicious."

Fred grudgingly took the card—anything to get away from this guy—and he moved to the other end of the bar. And then a little later, he grew concerned as he saw two men in dark suits escorting Martin out the front door.

Fred didn't know what was going on, but he figured it was time for him to get the hell out of there. But before he left—and against his better judgment—Fred glanced down at the business card Martin had given him. On the front of the small card, above two telephone numbers, were the words: the Brotherhood for the Understanding, Legitimization, and Legalization of the Subspecies of Human and Interplanetary Travelers.

Fred let out a huff. It all became clear to him then, and he shook his head and laughed. "Just as I thought," he said, and with that he pitched the card across the bar.

"It was all B.U.L.L.S.H.I.T!"

MADAM BLOTSKY

"Now, if you would, Mr. and Mrs. Bogue, please join hands to form the sacred circle, and we can begin." Madam Blotsky smiled in her artificial and patronizing way at the earnest young couple occupying the other two chairs at the table. This was their third séance in the past month, and she knew that Angelica and Earnest Bogue were now familiar with her procedures, so there was no need for her to expound upon the details. She could just get the show on the road, so to speak.

Everyone had gathered in the first floor room of a large old Victorian, located on the outskirts of Sleepy Hollow. It was certainly an interesting place for a medium's residence. One couldn't ask for better. And the couple thought that this was probably not by accident. Sleepy Hollow had its own reputation in the realm of the supernatural. And the house being located here, tended to give Madam Blotsky some credence.

The couple was told that this house was Madam Blotsky's home as well as her place of business, and that this séance room, off of the front hall, had been her dining room at one time. The walls of the séance room were covered by old-fashioned floral wallpaper and dark oak wainscoting. There was a rather impressive chandelier, currently unlit, hanging in the center of the ceiling, surrounded by black, pressed, tin tiles. A small circular table had been placed under this chandelier, in the center of the room, for the purpose of the séance. It was covered with a large brocaded tablecloth that hung over the sides and swept to the floor. Along one side of the room, in the wall at the front of the house, was a large window that would have brightened the room, but for the heavy draperies that were pulled tight across it, shutting out any light from the outside. The doorway to the front hall had been sealed with a stout oaken sliding door. The room was deliberately made as dark as possible, and, therefore, it was difficult to make out the peripheries. With only three candles burning in the center of the small round table, the edges of the room were left to the gloom.

As per the instructions from the previous gatherings, the three sat for a moment in silent meditation, waiting for Madam Blotsky to begin. The medium—for that was how Madam Blotsky presented herself—took a deep breath and recited her usual opening lines. "May the Devine Spirit be with us as we reach out to those who have crossed over the threshold between life and death. May He give us the wisdom to understand and heed the words of our dearly departed. May we be enlightened and uplifted. At this time, we call upon the spirit of Grace Brody, the beloved mother of Angelica Bogue. Please move among us and communicate with us. We implore you. We are here with open hearts and open minds. Join us and speak to us."

After several tense moments, the medium slumped forward in her seat and began to exhale in raspy and ragged breaths. The Bogues glanced, surreptitiously, at each other across the brocade covered table and then at the draperies that had begun to sway ominously as if a wind had just passed through the room.

Then, with a sharp inhalation, the medium jerked her head up in a sudden movement and, with a shuddering sigh, her eyes rolled back into her head. White orbs looked eerily from her ash hued face. Her thin scraggly gray hair floated above her head in a static halo, as if she was in the presence of a churning Tesla coil. Then, after presenting this ghastly visage to the sitters, the medium spoke in a soft feminine whisper, "Is that you, Angelica? It's me, dear. It's Mother. I'm here with you."

"Mother, is that you?" The young woman, Angelica Bogue, said in a plaintive voice. "At last, we have made the connection. I knew it. I knew you would speak from the grave. You always told me you would. You had such a close connection with the spirit world." The young woman gave her male companion another quick glance and continued talking. "I want you to know that Earnest and I love you, Mother. And we miss you, desperately."

The medium continued in a soft whisper. She appeared to be in a deep trance. "It does not end with death, my dear. Our lives, in your plane, are just one stage in the great cycle. I returned to tell you that. And to warn you, that what you do in this life will have repercussions in the next. I, myself, need to make amends for the errors I have committed in life. I will not rest if you do not help to right the wrongs that I have done. I need to ask you to, please, help me give meaning to the life I left behind. Will you help me?"

Angelica looked sidelong at Earnest and gave him an almost imperceptible nod. "Of course we want you to find peace and to honor your life. We'll do anything you ask. How can we help you, Mother? What is it that you would like us to do?"

Madam Blotsky dragged in several ragged breaths then spoke in the fragile voice of an old woman. "I would like you to make a donation in my name. The money I left behind must go to a higher purpose. I need to have this done, so I can find peace, so I can find eternal rest. Will you do this for me, Angelica? Will you help your own mother find eternal peace?"

"We love you, Mother," Angelica said. "We'll do anything you want with that money. It was your money after all. To whom shall we make this donation?"

Madam Blotsky rolled her head from side to side. She moaned as if she were feeling pain or great sorrow. Then she continued in the same soft whisper, "You know, I always believed in the afterlife, and I believed that we all have the ability, after death, to speak from the other side. I should have done more, while I lived, to encourage this communication. I regret that I failed to do my part. Please, in my name, make a donation to the local Psychic Church Society. It doesn't matter which one. Help others to find the bridge that connects our worlds."

The medium slumped forward as though she were exhausted and sat immobile for several minutes. At last, she raised her head and gazed distractedly around the room. "Were we successful this time? Did we reach your mother on the other side, Miss?" she asked in a weak voice.

"Yes, yes, thank you," the young woman gushed. "We have a lot to think about, don't we, Earnest?"

Angelica got up from the table and, after paying Madam Blotsky the agreed upon fee, she and Earnest said their goodbyes and departed.

"So, did you find anything out about the Psychic Church Society?" Angelica Cook asked as she entered the office that she shared with her fellow researcher, Earnest Sandford, at the Para-psychology Research Center at Albany State College, New York.

Earnest sat at a cluttered desk, staring fixedly into the computer screen that stuck up out of an intimidating pile of paper scattered across the surface of the desk. He gave Angelica a quick glance and motioned her over to a chair just behind his.

"I found out, that there is only one Psychic Church Society in the Eastern US. So, if we were to donate your 'inheritance' to any Psychic Church Society, it would have to be to this one." Earnest showed her the information on his computer screen. "It's administered by three individuals: Rutherford Stuart, A. J. Kriech, and Alice Jones. And that is very interesting indeed because, the last name on that list, Alice Jones, is in actuality, the legal name of our medium, Madam Blotsky. So by donating to this, so-called, society, we would, of course, be giving the money to Madam Blotsky and her cohorts. It's quite plain what this supposed medium had hoped to accomplish—as if paying her an exorbitant fee for the séance wasn't extortion enough."

Angelica picked up the stack of photos Earnest had lying on the edge of the desk. They were the pictures Earnest had taken under the heavily draped table during the séance with a selfy stick and a low-light camera. It was plain, the medium had an incriminating array of electronics and mechanical contraptions secreted under the tablecloth. One picture showed the hand of Madam Blotsky actually triggering one of them. Caught red-handed, as it were.

"It's one thing to rip people off with the false hope of contacting their loved ones, but it's really low to use someone's grief and vulnerability to extort even more money." Angelica dropped the photos back onto the desk. "I might have believed her—that voice and her trance face were very convincing—if my own mother wasn't actually alive and living in Florida. This Madam Blotsky is a real slime, a total fake."

"Yes, yes, she is. Doesn't care how she manipulates other people's emotions, or how she deceives them. Not much of a conscience there. And that's why, in her case, I'm going to call in Harry." Earnest smiled wickedly at Angelica, crossed his arms, and leaned back in his chair, defying Angelica to argue with him. "I think she deserves to get some of her own medicine."

Surprising him, the young woman didn't desist. "It's your call, Earnest. I won't argue. These swindlers make me sick. They make it impossible for genuine mediums to get any credibility. So, if you feel it's warranted, I say go for it."

Earnest nodded. He felt this Madam Blotsky should get what she had coming to her. Besides, he always got such a kick out of inflicting a little Harry on the wicked.

───※───

For the third time since she got home, Alice Jones, AKA Madam Blotsky, checked her computer for any sign of a deposit in the

Psychic Church Society's bank account at Greater New York Trust and Loan. Her home was not the old Victorian in Sleepy Hollow where she worked her scam. That house was, technically, owned by the Society, and so it had three owners: Stuart, Kriech, and herself. This home, a cute bungalow in New Rochelle, was hers alone.

She thought back on the last séance she had with the bogues. She believed it had gone extremely well. She was sure she had hooked the Bogue couple with her fake trance routine. She could always tell when she had someone completely bamboozled, and she knew she had played her role perfectly. She had been so sure the gullible pair had thought their mother required this donation to rest in peace, that she figured they would have rushed right home to do dead mommy's bidding, and that they'd be transferring funds to the Society Immediately. But, so far, nothing. Perhaps, they had had some kind of a hold up with their lawyer, or something.

Even so, that should not be too much of a problem, since the Psychic Church Society was listed as a non-profit organization, and a donation to something non-profit was always understandable after a death. It wasn't like she'd asked them to put the money into Madam Blotsky's personal account. That would have sent up a red flag. But giving it to the Society looked innocuous enough. Everyone gave to non-profits. Of course, the Society never did any non-profit work, no research, or good works of any kind. And, in truth, it wasn't a non-profit at all, since the monies went directly into the pockets of the administering officers. But, on the books, it was a charitable organization.

Breathing a reluctant sigh, she decided that she'd check again tomorrow. If nothing showed up in the account by then, she'd give the Bogues a few more days, and then she'd follow up with a discreet phone call. She wasn't going to let this fish get away.

She turned off her computer and the room went dark. Darker than it should have, actually, for it was still early evening, and it was May. Alice looked around the room, confused. Then she rubbed at her eyes. *I must have been staring at that computer too long*, she thought. *And my eyes are tired.* But after removing her hands from her eyes, she saw that the room did not brighten. If anything, it got darker still.

"What the hell!"

She could hardly make out anything in the room. She was beginning to wonder if there wasn't something seriously wrong with her eyes. Then she, finally, did see something at the other end of the room. There was a light, of some sort, over in the corner. It was faint at first, and then it grew brighter and larger. She stared in stunned perplexity. Then she squinted her eyes to try and make out some feature within the glow, curious to see just what the hell it was.

As she concentrated, she saw that it was taking on the shape of a person, and she could almost make out a face. Now, she was becoming concerned. *This can't be good,* she thought. "Who are you? What do you want?"

To her surprise and immense distress, she received an answer. "I...am the ghost of Harry. I have been summoned to your side."

Wow, she thought, *a real ghost.* "I must have actually managed to bring back a spirit," she said aloud. "Cripes! I didn't mean it. Go away! Go back to where you came from. I un-summon you!" Alice was starting to shake with fear. All these years she had pretended to call up ghosts, but she didn't really believe it could be done. Apparently, the spirits must have actually been listening to her.

"I have not come in answer to your summons," the ghost said in an eerie voice. "For you do not have the ability to summon. I am here at the behest of the many spirits you pretended to call. They are distressed that you have manipulated their loved one's grief to swindle them out of their rightful inheritance. They have joined together in their displeasure and demand retribution."

The ghost's voice seemed to come from everywhere, not just the corner where the glow was now taking on a more substantial form, though she could still see right through it. And as it coalesced and became more opaque, the wraith seemed to take on a face she thought she recognized, a familiar face from the past. *Was it?* "You can't be," she said. "You can't be. You said your name was … Harry?"

"That's right. And I have come to demand redress for the wrongs you have done. I spent a good portion of my life ferreting out the bogus mediums who prey on desperate mourners, the evil extortionists who swoop in, like vultures, to pluck the spoils from hapless, grieving victims. The swindlers. The goldbricks. The con-artists, like yourself. Believe it, Rosabelle. Believe."

Alice was now in paroxysms of terror. She was afraid that at any moment she might actually soil herself. "What do you want of me?" she choked out between gasps. "What can I do to make you go away and never come back?"

Harry's voice rang through the room like thunder. "I will return every evening until the day you die. But never, of course, when you try to summon me. Oh, no. You will only ever see me when you are alone. And I intend to make my visits more frightening with each passing day. Unless ..." The ghost's eyes took on a terrifying intensity.

"Unless?" Alice croaked. She was sure she was about to faint.

"Unless," the ghost of Harry continued. "You give up pretending to be a medium. ... And you give up extorting money from others, in any form. ... And you, in turn, make a considerable donation to a true non-profit organization that investigates paranormal activities."

"I will. I will." Alice covered her face with her hands, weeping from relief. There was a way out of this hell. Thank God!

※

Alice was left alone that evening to consider her sins and to repent. But, after a night of fitful sleep, she decided she must have dreamed the whole thing, or she must have suffered a small breakdown. But, at any rate, she figured she'd get over it, and the very next day, she promptly went right back to the old Victorian house in Sleepy Hollow to take up her ruse as the medium, Madam Blotsky. It was the only profession she knew, after all, and, because she made good money at it, it was hard to give it up.

Then later, that very night, Harry came for a second visit, and this one was truly frightening. Alice actually did manage to soil herself during this visit, but she convinced herself, she could tough it out. She deluded herself into thinking, she might be able to use these visits to her advantage. But each successive visit became, more and more, terrifying. And, finally, after five visits,

Alice feared for her sanity and, in self-defense, swore to give up pretending to be a medium.

Since she proved true to her word, the visits from Harry ceased.

༺༻

"I have some good news for you, Angelica," Earnest said with a light tone, as his associate entered the small, out-of-the-way, office at the Albany State College in New York. He seemed very perky today, unusual for him. He was usually serious of nature, a dedicated researcher, but today there was definitely a sparkle in his eye.

"Did our research grant come through?" Angelica asked, starting to get a little excited herself. The finances for their parapsychology research were starting to wear thin; they'd been waiting to hear news of the grant for months now.

"No, haven't seen anything on that, yet. But our research project has come into some money," he answered brightly. "And a substantial amount, too."

"Really, from where?"

"We were given a large donation from the Psychic Church Society. What do you think about that?"

"Well, I'd say, that was appropriate. I guess old Harry came through, huh?" Angelica sat in the chair just behind Earnest and looked over his shoulder at the computer screen and the list of new donations displayed there; then she gave Earnest a reproachful look.

"Oh, come on," he said. "You know Harry enjoys taking down these frauds. It was his vocation in life, after all, second only to his career as an escape artist. And, thankfully, for the benefit of our organization, he is still on the job, even after his death."

"All's well that ends well, eh, Earnest? I suppose you're right." Angelica usually didn't approve of harassing the fake mediums, and the Harry tactic *was* a bit 'shady', but she couldn't argue with the results.

ABOUT THE AUTHOR

Terry Daly Karl was born in Western New York and currently lives in Akron, New York. After studying psychology and philosophy at the University of Buffalo, she worked for the US Post Office as a postmaster for ten years.

Karl has always been fascinated by the unknown and unexplained, and she channeled that fascination into her first book, *Surrounded by Stones: A Ghost Story*.

Made in the USA
Middletown, DE
19 October 2022